THE PARTISANS AGAINST THE NAZI WAR MACHINE

A Documentary Novel

By

Hyman Shenkman

JONATHAN DAVID PUBLISHERS
Middle Village, N.Y. 11379

Library of Congress Catalogue Card No. 78-164516
ISBN 0-8246-0123-8

Printed in the United States of America

This Book Is Dedicated

To the people who died in Nazi camps, but remain alive in our hearts.

To the heroic partisans who dared to refuse SS orders, and placed their lives in deadly balance against the heavy odds in order to save their dignity and the lives of others.

To the Russian people who paid the highest price in blood to crush Nazism, the deadliest cancer of the twentieth century.

To the people of the United States who fought Nazism and gave a helping hand in finding a new home for its survivors.

To the State of Israel who opened all doors for its suffering people: the poor, the weak, the sick.

This is a tribute to all those who defied death in order to survive the holocaust and who stay on guard to prevent a rebirth of Nazism.

Author's Note

THREE DECADES have passed since the defeat of Nazism. Those who faced it at its height will never forget it. I'm one of them.

As long as the dangerous Nazi ideology still pollutes the air on several continents, the world must be told and retold about its biggest enemy on earth. It must learn from the lesson of horror and avoid its repetition.

There are those who will say, "Who wants to hear other people's problems? We have enough of our own." There are those who would rather share happiness with the lucky ones, than a tragic past with the depressed; dance instead of talking about tragedies; sing instead of voicing concern. And who wouldn't?

But there are those who say, "I fought Nazism in the Second World War and I'll fight it again if necessary. I'll proudly stand among those who fight for the abolition of the treacherous ideology which almost destroyed humanity."

Simon Wiesenthal, a Viennese who dedicated himself to bringing Nazi criminals to justice, once said: "I'm among those who believe in an after-life. There will come a time when we will be asked by the victims, 'What did you do after we left you in Germany?' Some will say, 'Well, I went to America and made a good living.' 'I,' he said, 'would like to add, I was thinking of you too.' "

There is more to it than showing up once a year to a memorial service, laying a wreath and making a prayer.

The wish of the victims, had they been given a chance to write it down, would probably read: "Remember us. Fight Nazism so that our great grandchildren and our people will never again be murdered."

How can anyone forget the tragedy?

A child killed by a shark while swimming in shallow waters will make the front pages. The tragedy will disturb millions, but not for long. The next day when the child's death is brought up, the public will say, "How about that? Isn't it too bad?" A week later they will have forgotten the child's name. A year later they will have forgotten the whole story. But the grieving parents never do, because the child was, and will always remain, a part of them. They will always be on guard, so it does not happen again to other children.

This book is not about a single child, but about six million people. A third of a people is the equivalent of three towns the size of Detroit. One-third for the United States would mean seventy million; for China a third would be 300 million, which is the whole population of the United States, England and France combined.

I want my American born son, his children, and millions of others like him, while reading this book, to put themselves in our place.

Can all good things in life be taken for granted?

As bad as some claim to have it—could it be worse?

My book doesn't cry for revenge. I don't want a tooth for a tooth or an eye for an eye. This would bring me no satisfaction. My heart goes out for those who wanted to walk, talk and laugh, as you and I on this blessed earth, instead of being buried under it. As one of the lucky ones who survived the holocaust, I have the right to hate. But I try not to; hate is self-defeating.

In this book, I am not seeding hatred. The happenings will speak for themselves.

I am not agitating, only exposing a truth which stands on its own merits.

v

I once heard a good Christian say, "The cross has two directions. The vertical line which points up to God and the horizontal line pointing to your fellow man."

"I believe in the horizontal line of the cross," he said, "since by helping my fellow man I'm already serving God."

While we are doing all right in the vertical direction we often neglect the horizontal. I'm talking about the moral obligation of those in power, who lent little or no help to a people who suffered for 2000 years, and whose suffering reached a climax under Nazism.

There are different reasons which motivate one to write a book. Mine is a moral obligation to expose the record of Nazism.

We are so wrapped up in ourselves, *our* home, *our* children, *our* future, that we often forget who we are: ordinary human beings rushing through a lifetime without taking a good look behind us.

We go to our places of worship, we read the lines in our prayerbooks, and we feel consoled and justified. Our religious leaders deliver fine sermons. We listen attentively; we agree and even identify ourselves with the words being spoken. Then it's over. We shake our preacher's hand, exchange smiles, good wishes, and then—out of sight, out of mind.

We go right back to our daily way of life with its overflow of plenty.

There have been many books written about the dangers of Nazism, but not enough. If I succeed in exposing just a bit more of the Nazi menace; if only one of my lines will serve as a fence, a barrier against this danger—my book will have made its contribution.

HYMAN SHENKMAN

March 1971
Southfield, Mich.

THE PARTISANS
AGAINST THE NAZI
WAR MACHINE

1

DAVID RAN FOR THE TRAIN, his legs driving him with some new powerful strength. It would be the last train, people said. David, as long as he lived, would never forget how he ran. It was as if the sound of his feet was impressed in his memory, in his muscles, as it rose from the pavement.

That morning the cry had gone up: "The Germans! The Germans are coming!"

David was at school when the cry went up, and he ran home. No one was there. They had all discussed it before, prepared for this moment. Things had long been uneasy in Poland. No one expected permanent peace between the Germans and the Russians. Someday one or the other would move, with Poland between them to be crushed. They had discussed this.

With the Germans, there would be no chance for Jews like David and his family. There was only one place to escape. To the East? Russia? Some were afraid to part with their homes, possessions; others didn't have much confidence in the Reds. It was a gamble. But it was the only chance.

When David found the house empty, he assumed the others had already left. This is how they had planned it. They would go together if they could; alone if they must.

1

So he took a few things he might need and he ran for that last train.

David's brother, Aaron, had gone that morning to a village some miles east. He was on the road, hurrying home, looking for David and his parents when German paratroopers appeared on the road and took him prisoner.

Some miles east of David's home, in Wilno, in a small Russian farming village, Natasha went about her chores, clucking at the animals and humming a little song.

Already the young men of her village had gone off to train for war. It seemed to her that everyone wore their worries on their faces.

But nothing had happened to them yet, so there still was time to hum.

2

IT SEEMED TO DAVID that he and everyone else in Wilno had been running from the moment the alarm was sounded. Thousands fled. Many went east on foot. Some had bicycles. Here and there an old cart, heaped with bedding and strung with old pots and pans, blocked the road. Far in the distance huge planes could be seen dropping parachutists. Polish soldiers, their weapons discarded, ran for the same exits as the people.

All day—running, running, running.

Birds were flapping their wings, perhaps wondering why all those creatures on the ground were shoving and pushing, when there was so much space a little higher up; while the people envied the birds, who flew so free in that fresh air in all directions, unconcerned with what kind of government they were going to live under.

The good Lord has made birds chirp rather than talk; and they need not communicate with people who shoot and kill all living things including themselves.

Like an airplane, they turned their wings, swooping down for closer observation of those thousands of two-legged creatures. Where were all those people going? The season is not over yet . . . all those bundles of food, yet they looked so insecure . . . when one worm will do for a bird.

3

David reached the depot just as the last train, already jammed with people, began to pull out. David ached. He could not breathe. Yet his legs would not stop; not now.

His legs carried him past those who could not make it, then down the track. His eyes fixed on the step of the last boxcar. It seemed the only spot not taken. On he went— the poorest runner in his school, but now like a champion. On, though his head sagged and his eyes watered.

He stumbled, but he went on. Now the last step was filled. Someone had taken the last space. But that did not defeat him. A dozen more were ahead of him, their eyes on the same wooden step.

Ten feet now and he began to shout, "Make more room! Make more room! There are more who want to go!"

A few inched forward, and a small bit of step showed itself. In a moment, David was up.

A dozen people jammed the little steps. They stood as if frozen, as if their feet were nailed to the warped boards underneath them. The smell and heat and sweat of fear covered them all.

The wheels began to turn faster now. A whistle screamed. For a moment, David had the feeling that the train was not moving, only the tracks were.

From the platform came the cries of those who could not get on.

A middle-aged man grabbed the coat of a boy on the step and screamed at him, "Move! Squeeze! You bastard!" The boy closed his eyes and held tighter, tighter to the rail. Then he let go, and the man pulled him off and took his place.

The boy fell to the ground, crying in a horrible way. Then he was gone, and David could no longer hear him.

Another boy took his place—a little boy hardly able to take another step. He walked, wobbling like a duck, lost. Up ahead, a woman and a young girl screamed at the boy:

"Come, Mojshele, come! Don't give up. Hurry. Drop the bundle, Mojshele, and run."

But he could not hear them because of all the noise of

4

those being left behind. Then he was swallowed up in the crowd.

He reappeared, and now he was crying. Tears rolled down his cheeks.

Then he saw her and he ran toward the steps to which she and the girl were clinging.

"Please, please, good people," the mother implored. "Squeeze to make an inch for my baby. Just an inch." Two girls squeezed together. "A little more," the mother cried, "Save another life. A young life."

Someone picked the boy up and handed him to the mother who grabbed him with one hand as the train rolled by. For a moment the boy swung in mid-air at the end of his mother's arm. Then she pulled him to her.

The train rocked along now, at a steady pace, toward the east, and David lost himself in thought, wedged in among the mass of people.

David thought of the others now, of his family. Around him, on the steps, there was no noise. Everyone clinging there, everyone who had won a chance on the gamble, everyone was silent. All had left others behind.

It was the woman and the little boy, of course, who made him think of the others. The woman had drawn the boy to her. David remembered so many days, walking with friends, one boy's arm about the other, the warmth of it and the safety of it. He saw his father, sitting in his chair in the warmth of their home, reciting the tales of the ages. He saw the table set outside the house, during the festival when his father insisted that the family eat outside, like the first pilgrims on their way back to Israel.

David was twenty. Lean. Young. He stood there, packed tight against the sweat and smell and heaviness of all the others who sought life.

A foot touched his. The body pressed against his back moved, trying to change positions. He turned his head and looked over his shoulder. It was a girl; about eighteen. He pushed his body against the silent people around him, squeezing out a hair's more space for her.

"*Aciu*," she said.

The sound of the Lithuanian word rubbed against him, deep inside, in the same way as her body rubbed against his with every rock of the train.

"*Aciu.*"

How many times did the roughness of that same language speak hate, hate of the Jews, who, when they walked by the Gentile section of Wilno were called names.

Now the "thank you" murmured in this same language was soft and soothing.

David remembered how, when he was only seven, he had asked his mother why, if the Jews were so abused and hounded, why they were considered the Chosen People?

His parents could never answer. What was there to say?

Once his grandfather had grumbled, "Don't ask silly questions, child. Don't you know what we are chosen for? To be pushed on the street. To be spit at."

Even then, at seven, David knew his grandfather was right.

David had once walked with him on the street when two Polish youngsters walked by and pulled hard on the old man's beard. When his grandfather protested, he was told, "Shut up, you old Jewish puss."

At the same early age, David began to feel contempt. He saw a boy spit at a Jewish man old enough to be his grandfather. As he grew up, he heard more and more abuse, and was himself roughed up by complete strangers just because he was born of Jewish parents. In his home he was surrounded by a loving family; he learned hatred outside. He was taught and compelled to hate.

The feuding Poles and Lithuanians each claimed that the city of Wilno belonged to them. The Jews claimed nothing. All they wanted was to be left alone, to live their own culture, tradition and lives. The Jews of the city called it whatever its official name was, but world Jewry called it Vilne, the Jerusalem of Lithuania. The cradle and center of Jewish culture in Europe. Jews from all over the world sent their children to this city to study. Thousands were sent from overseas to learn Yiddish, Hebrew, the fine points of the Bible and the riches between the lines of the Torah.

6

David did not have to be told about resentment and persecution. One could learn it as soon as his eyes could see. It didn't require any intelligence. A child's common sense, his intuition told him and made him aware of this burden which he was born with and would die with.

At home he learned that he was a Jew. Outside he was called *Zyd* with disdain. David never felt guilty for being born a Jew, but he did feel guilty for not being able to avoid the harassment and, above all, he felt frustrated for having to swallow his pride.

At teen-age, he began to realize that the mutual resentment was so deeply imbedded in the people of Wilno that it was for many a way of life. He made an uneasy peace with it. He thought he learned to live with it.

There was hardly a day when he didn't encounter a slur as he passed a non-Jewish area on his way to school. With time, he came to think of this as normal.

David's parents sweated in the summer in their small, stuffy shoe store, and half froze during the winter. Tired from work, his father often fell asleep on the sofa, and had to be awakened by mother for dinner.

Now, as the train hurried as fast as it could to the East, David thought of his parents. He could not find them when the alarm was given. Had they been out looking for him? Had they been able to save themselves?

A soft sigh escaped from the girl behind him.

She was different from him. The very language she spoke reminded him of slurs and abuses so painful to him, the very things that had driven him and his people so close to each other, and away from the others.

Now they stood close, forced against each other by the evil now loose in Europe. In all the madness of that afternoon, only the touch of her against his back bespoke of humanity.

7

3

THE TRAIN WENT SLOWLY over old, shaky rails. Its rattles seemed to say kai, tai, ta tsi. It sounded like "bye, bye, Nazi."

The trees they passed had many of their branches broken, like so many families.

The train kept moving with people glued to every available inch, like flies to flypaper, but none trying to pull free.

They clung to the foot boards and handrails, with determination born of desperation. Their faces showed strain, mixed with emotion. Gradually, as they covered more and more mileage their faces became more drawn, and covered with dust. Short hair shivered like the bristles of a broom, long hair flew in all directions at the mercy of the wind.

No one talked. Who knew how many more such hours were left until the unknown destination? They saved every breath, every ounce of strength that was left.

They looked toward the engine slowly puffing away, or down at the clumsily turning wheels as if they were measuring every inch of movement. People could still hear the cries and prayers of those who didn't make the train. Heads sagged in sadness.

Suddenly the train began to slow down, and the planks between the rails became small vertical boards with a space between them. Finally the planks stood still and so did the train. The engine stopped and a sharp police whistle sounded from the front of the train.

"Messerschmidts are approaching!" a loud voice from a loudspeaker shouted. "Into the ditches!"

Some jumped off, others hesitated.

"Jump into the ditches, right now! It's an order!"

David turned around and looked at the blond, long-haired girl behind him. She was immobile. Afraid of losing her valuable step-spot, she had frozen, unable to move.

He grabbed her hand, and pulled her off the step. He ran with her as if she were chained to him; off the ramp and down a ditch. He pulled her ahead of him, and both stumbled falling flat, face down. They looked up and there were the three mysterious iron birds with the infamous black crosses on their wings. Their hands spontaneously clasped each other. He felt her cheeks press against his. Their eyes closed tight and their hearts stopped.

Then the deadly birds passed and they opened their eyes. For the first time they had an opportunity to take a real look at each other. She was pale but beautiful. He felt her thin hands tremble over his shoulders. They were too excited to talk. They looked into each others eyes with bewilderment.

She said, *"Aciu,"* again.

"You were a great help to me," she said. "I guess I just froze. They could have dropped a bomb and killed me."

"They must have saved it for someone more important," replied David.

The train engineer came out and said, "You may go down to the river and wash up. All be back here in a half hour."

People stretched legs and arms, and turned their heads both ways. All their joints felt stiff. A youngster rubbed his hands, to bring back the circulation. He tried to move his fingers, numb from clasping to the rail for hours.

A heavy set woman holding the hands of two children took a deep breath. Along with the others she was drenched with the perspiration of fear.

9

An old man with a long, white beard, black suit and hat walked slowly with a stick, staring down at the dusty road.

David saw an image of his grandfather in this old man. He turned to him and said: "So hot, and no rain. Thank God for that."

The old man raised his eyes, threw up his head toward Heaven and said, "With His help we'll survive yet."

Down the slope the crowd began to swell.

Mojshele was there with the mother and sister who had saved him. His sister was trying to make him stop crying while his mother washed the tears off his face. "Where is Daddy?" he kept asking. "We'll see Daddy, maybe tomorrow," his mother said with a voice short of confidence. It was one of the broken families; yet a family. So many refugees couldn't even claim that.

The blond girl turned to David.

"My name is Maria. What's your name?"

"David."

"Do you know where we are going?"

"Nobody knows."

"And I guess no one probably cares as long as it pulls us out of Hitler's claws."

"Where is your family, David?" Maria asked after a pause.

"In Vilnius," David said sadly.

"Vilnius," she said. "There I used to travel by horse and buggy from Vileika. I wonder what they are all doing now?" she choked up. "Maybe, I shouldn't have left them."

"Why did you?" asked David.

"I worked for the Red Administration. Germans would question me, and I would be arrested. Besides, I had no intention of giving away my friends and employees."

The crowd now was walking into the water. Hands scooped water into dry mouths. Faces felt the refreshing coldness of it. Maria raised her dress just above her knees and took a deep bend to reach for water.

When she had finished, she said to David, "A peaceful night after a hectic day. *Viskas bus geraj.* Everything will be okay."

10

David nodded.

She could feel, as did David, the differences between them, but this did not bother her. Suddenly, David had become to her a symbol of protection, brotherhood.

She knew they would not travel long together. They would be separated, David probably to the army, she somewhere else. But she was grateful that on this day of terror he had been there, to throw his arm about her in the ditch, to lead her off the train when she had been unable to move.

She knew David was Jewish even before he opened his mouth. She could always tell Jewish people. They dressed differently, even walked differently. She recognized his pale face which testified to harassments and persecutions for centuries. She could sense his distrust and resentment, because her people tried to put his people down.

They started back to the train.

David folded his towel, put it under his arm and with his head down began to walk slowly towards the train. Maria followed, pulling herself up to his side.

"I wonder where to now?" she asked.

David shrugged.

She opened a little bundle and offered David a piece of black bread. Hungry and tired, he hesitated for a while.

"Take it. I have some more. Don't worry. I bet you that tomorrow morning we'll wake up in a town far away and we'll get plenty to eat."

David managed a faint smile. The bread was a treat to him. It tasted like cake. "Thanks, is it home baked?"

"Yes."

As they approached the tracks they noticed a change.

Their train wasn't there. For a while they thought they were lost, but a militia man pointed in a direction several hundred feet away and kept repeating: "Board the box cars over there." The train was gone. It was needed for troop transportation.

"We are going to ride in box cars," David said to Maria. "Beggars can't be choosers."

Maria said, "As long as it moves." She put her hand on David's shoulder as she struggled into a high box car.

11

David followed. Inside it was all black from the powder of the unloaded coal.

People who had just washed and bathed in the river waters climbed into the dirty cars without protesting. It looked like a treat. Enough room to share, even to sit down. Some who had a bundle with them sat on it or put their heads on it. A few loud whistles from the train's engineer, a jolt or two, and the train went rolling along, slowly but surely, with the coal dust flying all around.

"Thank God," a woman murmured. "I can survive hundreds of these journeys but not one Hitler."

The starless night began to blend in closer with the black of the coal.

Children fell asleep, adults grew weary and lowered their voices. It became pitch dark; it was hard for some to see the time, but most cared less.

No one had to worry about going to work the next day; no one really cared where he was going, as long as it was away from the oncoming Nazis.

David stood up most of the night holding on to the side board with Maria.

Once she said, "With all that black dust flying, people might have a hard time recognizing each other. Remember, David, I have long blond hair and my dress is blue."

David couldn't resist a smile.

Soon talk all but disappeared. A few whispers from mothers trying to comfort their whining children were heard occasionally. But mainly there was the constant rattle of the wheels.

Only shadows could be seen of an elderly man lying sideways, a youngster sleeping soundly on his back, a mother sitting against the board with a child in her arms. Mothers never seemed to get tired as long as their children slept. Finally the whole boxcar became peaceful.

David, standing with hands grasping the side boards, kept looking at the silhouettes of the forest, while Maria did the same. Sporadic glances from her eyes focused on David's face.

What was he thinking about? Probably his family, his home . . . a girl friend. . . .

Unaware of her thoughts, David raised his head, stretched his arms out. He yawned and sat down. "I might as well call it a day."

"Me, too," Maria said. "Tomorrow is another day. A big day. We'll reach a city. We'll learn how many miles we are away from home."

David sank into deep thought. He paused for awhile.

"I'm worried about my parents. I ran home and didn't find them. Maybe they were looking for me. I doubt if they left town. They wouldn't have done it without finding me first. My only hope is that they couldn't find me and left on their own. Time will tell."

David made himself more comfortable. He tried to close one eye, then the other. He was too tired and chilly to sleep at first. Before he dozed off he felt someone cuddle in closer to him. It was Maria. This was the last he remembered.

He dreamed—dreamed of his parents trying to get on this box car. "Here, here! Pa, Ma, here! Here I am." He sat up with his hands stretched out and eyes open.

It was dawn. Maria, rubbing her bloodshot, coal-irritated eyes, looked at him, scared.

"David, you had a nightmare."

"Oh, no . . . No, I had a good dream . . . I saw my parents . . . It was so real. Why did you have to wake me up?"

"I didn't. You woke me up."

"Where are we anyway?"

"I heard someone mention Latupy."

"Are we behind the Russian border?"

"No," someone replied. "Latupy is a Polish border stop."

"Didn't you hear? We are to get off the train and walk across the Russian border and there look for further means of transportation."

4

PEOPLE STARTED DOWN the steep train ladder. Hungry, cold and scared, the children cried. A little girl with her teeth chattering held onto her father.

"Just wait here, my child. I'll go first and then help you down." Sleepily she embraced him with both hands, her cheek against his neck. He pulled her up, then set her on the ground. "Watch out, child, there is a broken bottle."

Young and old tripped, some fell over the unpredictable dark terrain. Finally they got to a country road.

"Which way? Which way?" they asked.

"Straight ahead, over the swamp," a voice sounded. "Line up in one row. Everybody follow me."

A heavy voice sounded from behind.

"What about food?"

"We are hungry," shouted an older, bearded man.

"I need milk for my baby," cried out a young mother, cradling her little one in her arms.

"There is no one around here to feed us," the first voice answered. "Let's get moving across the border. The Germans are at our heels."

The crowd surged toward the swampy area. Barefoot, with shoes in hands, hundreds were wading, rocking like fat geese.

14

David stepped on a sharp object and cut his toe. He hopped out of the water on one foot. He sat down.

Maria, who followed him like a shadow, was right by him. She pulled out a big, wrinkled handkerchief, bent down and said: "Let's see . . . you have a little piece of glass stuck there. Just hold still."

"Ouch," screamed David. Blood began to drip.

"It's all right," Maria told him in a reassuring voice. She wrapped his foot with her only handkerchief, twice the regular size and tied it. "Hold your foot up on my shoulder for a little while, until the blood settles."

They saw people joining the exodus. They heard names, Abram . . . Nathan. . . .

Some of the voices seemed petrified—"Where is Dad and Mom? Did you see Sarahle?"

People slowed down for a closer look, as two brothers who found each other in the dawn of a gray morning, threw arms about each other. No one else seemed to know them. Some nodded, wishing it had happened to them.

Time was too short and hectic to pause. Everyone had to move on as the weak and old moved up from the rear ranks. David tried to put his shoe on. It hurt, but he could continue.

Maria took him by the arm and helped him up.

"You are the first casualty," she said.

"Lucky I have a nurse on hand," replied David.

"Yeh, we made it this far, we'll overcome everything," said Maria with a soft yet determined motion of her hand.

They followed the leader through pine trees growing one atop the other. Bare feet received a rash from poison ivy.

"Wow," exclaimed Maria, "that hurts. That must be poison oak. I wonder why they call it poison when it itches and burns like fire."

"Like this world," said David, "just like the world."

She touched her foot and felt a group of welts breaking out all over. She rubbed it and it began to itch more.

"Now we have two invalids. How is your foot, David?"

"I'll live to be a hundred," he replied.

15

"The way things are going, I'll settle for fifty," quipped Maria.

Limping and hobbling, they still could stay ahead of the very old and the very young.

A grey-haired man with deep wrinkles showing the stress of the two-day ordeal sat near a weeping willow. Its branches sagged over him as if they were trying to tell him something. Its sad look reflected the feeling of this nearly hopeless man. At his side several people tried to give him encouragement.

C'mon Grandpa, try to get up . . . C'mon; you just can't stay here."

"Go on children," he said, "don't wait for me. You can still save yourselves. You still have a long life ahead of you."

"We can't leave you here in no man's land, you know we can't. There is no one here to help you. The Germans will come and finish you off."

"Go children, go . . . I just can't get up . . ."

"Put your arm around me, Pa," a mustached middle-aged man ordered.

"C'mon Grandpa, we'll carry you over the border, it couldn't be far now," said a youngster with a changing voice.

A pull, a lift and up he went over the shoulder of his son.

"Just take it easy, Pa," remarked a husky man, who just came up to the scene. "We'll take turns."

Another youngster in a school cap said, "We wouldn't leave you now."

A coyote and hyena sang out in a distant duet hoping for someone to be left for them. But their chances were slim. More and more men, boys and even girls offered to help. When the exhausted man couldn't stand up, people in turn grabbed his arms and legs and carried him. Breathing with difficulty, he stared at the people flocking around him, waiting for their chance to help him.

David said to Maria, "Look at the new friends he is

16

getting. If he could only get new strength—see how human hearts open up when a man is in trouble."

The human caravan was moving down a valley. Like geese they were following a leader who wasn't sure himself whether he was going in the right direction.

Across a pasture and over a low rail fence people began to climb. On the other side there were helping hands available. It became obvious, that as the march went on, people became closer, Jew to Gentile. For centuries, they had lived in ghettos, spoke their own languages, with little contact and understanding. Now they were like one big family.

All of a sudden, in less than two days, they learned that there is one goal for all, the same goal: holding on to precious life.

Maria was the first one to notice it.

"Life is so sad and yet I feel a spark of joy in my heart when I see people behaving like people. Look, David, at the Pole taking the little Jewish girl from her mother and putting her up on his shoulders. And did you see the Jewish man guiding a lost little girl who speaks Lithuanian? He can't even understand her, but does it matter?"

David said, "Let's hope the Russians will give us such a reception. My Dad used to say: Don't expect much and you'll never be disappointed. If the Russians will only give us something to eat, I'll be glad. I'm hungry like a wolf."

The lead column was approaching a steep hill. They stopped for a moment waiting for those who lagged behind, or perhaps just to take a breather.

It was just a hill, but to these exhausted people it looked as high as a mountain—a mountain with fenceposts atop it. And between the posts, wires. . . .

"Is that the border already?" a heavy-set woman with two children asked impatiently.

People looked for an answer, but nobody had one.

"My God," another woman said, "how far must we go?"

It was the border; and driven by their excitement and blinded by fear, people stumbled into the wire and fell back bleeding.

"How are we going to get through?" frustrated voices cried in chorus.

"We need men with canes, men with pocket knives! All men, quickly! We need your help."

Several dozen men came from all directions. The rest of the column watched them, hopefully.

It wasn't easy. With no tools and little know-how, it wasn't a simple thing to take apart something that had been put together with proper equipment by a capable engineering corps.

There were many "would-be" engineers, but not one of them really knew how.

"You may fiddle with your sardine can opener from here to eternity," a refugee said. "Let's get the stick between the wires."

People sat down on the dewy ground and watched the growing number of men frantically trying to break down at least one post. David limped over to see what he could do.

One husky man got hold of a heavy stone and banged it against a stubborn post, which wouldn't budge. A man in a fireman's uniform tried to pull the wires down with towels covering both hands, and a young man dug behind rusty nails trying desperately to release a few wires. The people were weary; concerned, nervous and impatient.

"We can't stay here much longer; we'll starve to death."

"My baby is getting sick. Is there a doctor?"

No one answered.

The old man lay peacefully, a bundle supporting his head. He lay still and said nothing. "What is going to happen to us," someone asked. "What will happen to all of us will happen to you," came a reply.

"Funny, funny, very funny," the first voice said. "If you are a comedian, why can't you make me laugh?"

Some got on each others' shattered nerves; others accepted the sarcasms as a means of keeping up their morale. An exchange of insults followed and it turned into a name-calling contest.

"Oh God, my tooth is killing me. I just can't take it,"

said a bald, short old man with a grey beard and metal glasses. He sat with his head buried between his hands.

"Shut up, you old devil, you are not the only one here," a young man said. "There are others that suffer and yet keep quiet."

"You punk, who are you calling an old devil? You shouldn't live to be my age. . . . Oh, my tooth!"

"I don't care if you lose all your teeth but one; that should remain to give you a toothache."

People became aroused at the youngster's arrogance and disrespect.

"How dare you talk to your elder like that! Phooey! Sha! Don't forget he is old enough to be your grandfather. You be quiet."

The youngster lowered his head; his apple red cheeks began to turn pale. He turned away and went over to the bustling men. He pulled out a soup spoon and began to dig around a spot at the bottom of the post. He tried frantically, but when he saw that this border marker was deep and solid in the ground he stopped in disgust. He looked all over his pockets for something else. Finally he pulled out a box of matches, gathered a few odd papers and cloth around the pole and set it on fire.

"Put it out, idiot! . . . Put it out!" Confused and unsure of himself, he tramped his feet over the raging fire.

"Let us not do foolish things," a man said. "German planes are scouting this area. A fire at night is what they are looking for, to find the border and destroy all of us here."

"Everybody who has a spoon, a knife, come here! Let's work together in one section of the border instead of each one trying to be in business for himself. We are all going to dig the dirt from under the wires in this section. Time is against us so let's get to work, fellows. Let's get going!"

This man, dressed in a railway uniform, seemed to have common sense and leadership. He delegated authority among the men he considered to be more responsible.

"Those who have knives raise your hand. Good! Line

19

up from this post to the other post and start softening up the hard sand at the wire."

Men fell to their knees and while they were chipping away at the ground the railway man called again.

"Now whoever has a spoon, hand, fingernails, start digging the sand out toward you."

His order was obeyed with almost military readiness and in a few minutes the feverish work began to show fruits.

"We need more volunteers to give those men a breather," he shouted. "Here comes a man with a bulldozer." Not expecting to hear joshing from a serious man like him, everyone looked around for a moment, then burst into laughter.

"That would be nice, people, wouldn't it?" he went on. "But right now we are going to be human bulldozers ourselves. Hey, girls, I see you came to help. You can move that soft sand farther away from the wire."

"Let me have your jack knife for awhile, man, that's a life saver." He cut off a hard piece of bark and began to flatten out piles of the sand accumulated by the diggers, who were working on their knees with their hands throwing sand between their legs like beavers.

David and Maria were in the second shift. "Boy," she said. "This is what I call getting into Russia the hard way."

"If the Russians don't give us a job as sewer diggers they are wasting our talent," replied David.

Some people began to crawl under the wire to deepen the hole. A cheer from the people was heard when a boy stuck his head out from the other side of the wire.

"Hurrah, we are in the Soviet Union," exclaimed a young girl.

"Not yet," said the railman, "we still have to dig it bigger so we all can get through, and then maybe the next night the Nazis will fall in and bury themselves."

No one crawled over to the other side until the hole was large enough. Then a few emerged on the other side of the wire. Soon the rest struggled to their feet, picked up their few belongings and walked slowly toward the pit.

"No pushing folks, just line up, we are all going to make it over. Bend down a little more and watch the wires above," said the railman, unhooking a plump, clumsy woman who barely made it with her bundle tied to her back.

He looked around and found in the dark several silhouettes of people lying on the ground.

"Hey, wake up, folks. Wake up."

"What happened? Huh?" asked the awakened with big eyes open. "Where are we?"

"We are still in the same place. While you were sleeping we built an underground canal. C'mon, the rest of the crowd is already on Russian soil—and don't forget your bundles."

David and Maria were helping the confused ones to find their belongings. As they were about to help the older man with the toothache, someone pushed ahead of them to help. It was the young boy who had been rude and unkind earlier.

"Hold on, pops! In a minute or two you'll be in another country," the young man said. "How is your tooth?"

The old man recognized the youngster, took a side glance at him, and said nothing. He accepted the young man's help, but didn't forgive him. Not yet anyway. He was still peeved at him. With one hand on his stick and the other on his chin, the old man looked as if he were in deep pain. The whole journey was just too much for him. Perhaps more than he would have been able to take, under normal circumstances.

But when the youngster pulled him up from the pit, (now in Russia) the old man mumbled, "Thanks." He seemed to say: "Maybe tomorrow or the day after tomorrow, when I feel better, I may even talk to you."

People looked around but there was nothing in sight. Nothing but fields and fields, in front of a thick wood running along valleys and over hills from there to eternity.

There must be something behind those woods. A village, a house, a human soul, something.

The cry of a dog from a distance silenced the people. It sounded more like a coyote. The more attentively they listened the more it sounded like the cry of a child.

"Those are coyotes, all right," someone said. "A bad sign. They live far from people. Don't expect homes nearby."

"That means we may have to walk for another two days, to find shelter?" a distressed elderly lady carrying a handbag asked. "I just can't go on like this. I'm out of breath. My throat is dry."

Maria came up to her and handed her an apple and said, "There, ma, try this. Let me hold the bag for you." After the lady sank her teeth into the apple, Maria said: "C'mon lady, try to keep up. It won't take long. See this forest? Right behind it we are going to find a big village. People will be coming out with bread and salt. Boy, will I be drinking away that water from the well. . . ."

"I wish you were right, good girl, because I just can't take it any more."

They crossed field after field, then entered the woods. When the trees began to thin out, when every step seemed lightened by the hope that now they had found safety, the bullets rang out.

5

"NO! NO!" SOMEONE SHRIEKED from the column of refugees. "No! We are civilians!"

The gunfire trickled off, then stopped altogether. People surged toward a little girl who was screaming in pain. She held her arm, but her fingers could not stop the blood.

Her mother's screams pierced the air and seemed to echo for miles.

"My child! My baby! She's shot! Help her! Help her!"

David was a few feet away from the child. He ripped off his shirt, wrapped it around the wound, and tied the sleeves.

"Okay," he said to the child. "You'll be all right. You're okay now."

The child's cries became whimpers, and the mother wiped her tears. "Thank God," the mother said, "it is only an arm."

Indeed, she was luckier than another. There was a sudden commotion on the other side of the group, where someone had come across a boy who had taken a bullet in the stomach.

In their panic, no one saw him fall. No one heard him shout.

Now he lay there, gasping for air desperately and

23

moaning. People hurried about, ready to help. But no one knew what to do.

"Is there a doctor?" someone shouted.

A man tried to breathe air into the boy's mouth, but it did not help. Someone wiped his face, but immediately it was full of death sweat again.

No one claimed him as son or nephew. He apparently had come alone, and was among strangers. Now, he was going to die alone, among strangers. The woman brushed his face gently once more. Then people began moving away.

Russian soldiers appeared with guns level at their waists. Someone shouted, "Here is a girl shot in the arm, and there lies a boy dying."

An army nurse with a red cross on the sleeve of her coat pushed through to the girl. She poured something over the wound, and placed a real bandage over it.

Then she went over to where the boy lay alone, silent now. She half bent over him, then straightened and returned to the troops.

Now a voice of command rang from amidst the soldiers. "Everybody," it said, "hands up!"

Soldiers with bayonets walked toward the refugees and stopped fifty feet away, their faces firm, their eyes piercing. Their leader said to them, "All right. They are civilians."

Then, to the refugees, he ordered:

"Everyone line up! Put your bundles at your feet. All firearms, knives, razors, hatchets, picks and other sharp objects must be laid out in front of your bundles."

"You have two minutes time. Anyone who fails to obey will be shot."

People hurried to obey. They opened their little bags and began to look for anything that might be sharp. Pocket knives, razor blades, and even an opener for a sardine can fell to the ground in front of the officer.

A lady dropped a fork and a spoon in front of her bundle.

"Why the spoon?" another refugee asked her.

"That spoon has such a crazy edge it scratches my tongue," the woman replied. "Now let them try it. Besides,

24

after I have come this far, should I be shot because of a kitchen spoon?"

David looked at the spoon and said, "She is right. She has used it for digging, and now it is sharp."

Maria smiled, and whispered, "Let them have the spoon. But don't tell them what we did with it. Let them guess."

The voice of the officer cut in: "You have one minute," and talk stopped as the search of bundles was stepped up again.

The old man who had complained about his toothache was so excited, his artificial teeth nearly fell out as he bent over his bundle.

The "dangerous weapons" were scooped by soldiers into their helmets. Then the officer in charge, who had a cigaret in one hand and a notebook in the other, stepped closer to the refugees and said, "Who is your leader?"

The refugees looked at each other in bewilderment.

"You have no leader?" the officer asked.

"The railman," someone said. "The man in the train uniform."

Piasecki stepped forward.

"Your name?" the officer asked.

"Josef Piasecki."

"Your papers?"

"Here," said Piasecki, bringing a hand out of his coat.

The Russian turned on a flashlight and pondered the papers for a long time. The refugees were silent as death.

Now the Russian raised his eyes again to Piasecki.

"I heard a language that sounded like German," he said, "so I ordered the shooting. I thought it was a German patrol."

"Why didn't you cross the border by a normal channel at the gate?"

David was struck wildly by the question. He wanted to laugh. What gate? What normal channel was there for the refugee?

The Russian went on, "The gate is a few miles from here. Why didn't you let anyone know who you were before you jumped a national border?"

The officer did not get an answer. Nor did it seem that he expected one. People knew what he meant by a language that sounded like German. He had heard the refugees speaking Yiddish.

Neither did he apologize for the dead boy or the wounded girl. He was a professional. He regarded the casualties as the kind of accident that is unavoidable in war.

He addressed Piasecki again.

"See this hill? Turn to the left and go around it. There is a village, Leninskoje. I will send a soldier with you with an order to the village elder to settle you overnight in a barn."

"What about food and water?" Piasecki asked. "Some of these people haven't eaten in two days. Children have had no milk."

The lieutenant regarded him again with that professionalism.

"Do you know what time it is? Close to three o'clock in the morning. I can't wake the collective farmers now to feed you. They have to get up and go to work in three hours. Tomorrow we'll see to it that you'll be fed before you move on further. This is a battle zone, and only people who are approved may stay here."

This seemed to satisfy the refugees.

Away, toward the hill they moved, like a caravan of used-up people. They did not complain as they went over the slopes and down a narrow path. They seemed, now that they were over the border, to have no more energy for talk. At the end of the narrow path, they came to the barn.

"No smoking in here," the soldier said. "No smoking. Just lay down on the hay and be quiet."

Like flies after a storm, the people dropped into the hay. In a few minutes everyone was asleep.

They slept for several hours, but to them it seemed only minutes before they were awakened by a loud voice.

"Josef Piasecki! Who is Piasecki?"

When their leader had shaken himself awake, the soldier

who had called said, "Get your people outside. Line them up. Get them in order. You are going to be fed."

The people quickened at the mention of food. It seemed to awaken memories. With Piasecki urging them on, they got their things together and lined up outside the barn.

Many now saw Piasecki really for the first time.

He was of stocky build, and he had a pleasant face trimmed with a little black mustache. He seemed always on the go, tending to this and to that. He showed concern, and he was constantly listening to someone's problems.

Everyone responded to him, and a bond was cast between them and him. By the next day, he was Josef to all of them, and it was obvious how much they liked him. His name was heard a hundred times a day and more.

He was the people's commander—and their father, mother, and brother.

A boy in the line cried. The border wires had scratched his arm deeply the night before, and now it began to burn.

David pulled off his sweatshirt, tore off a strip of cloth, and bandaged the scratch.

He said to Maria, "I'm not worried about the shirt. Soon I'll be drafted anyway. I'll be dressed from head to toe in a new uniform."

"Do you have relatives in Russia?" Maria asked.

"No," he said.

Then he asked her, "What will you do now that we are here, Maria?"

"I'm going to volunteer as a nurse, so I can help nice boys like you."

"Why did *you* run from the Nazis?"

"For the same reason you did, David."

"That cannot be," said David. "You see, I am a Jew. I had to run. There is no chance for a Jew under the Nazis. But why did you have to escape? Were you by chance a member of the Communist youth group?"

"Yes," she said. "But this was not my only reason."

"You are not sorry you left home?"

"Sorry? The last few days have changed my life. I've learned to get to like people."

27

"Did you hate people?" David teased.

"Not exactly," she said. "I was just afraid of them, especially the boys."

David waited for her to go on, but she didn't. She felt she had said too much already. She remembered, in that instant, that she had only known David two days.

"What's wrong with boys?" David pressed.

"Nothing, David," said Maria. "I'm sorry I brought it up. If I tell you that in two days I have talked more to you than to any boy in my lifetime, would you believe me?"

David was going to say no, but something about the way she looked, and the sound of her voice, made him refrain.

He decided not to press any more. To him, it was no more than a temporary companionship. In peacetime they could not talk like this. They would live in separate ghettos, following entirely different ways of life.

Now, in war, they saw each other today and walked together and talked. Tomorrow? David fully expected that they would be separated tomorrow or the next day or the next and would never meet again.

He could never think of marrying Maria. His parents, family, friends—none of them would ever approve or recognize it. Their customs, their manners and above all their religions were incompatible.

He could never see himself married to anyone who could have considered him a Christ-killer. When harassed, as a teen-ager and even now, he would tell his taunters: "I was not there at that time. I want no part of it, and I want no part of you."

At first, David had felt uncomfortable talking to Maria. It seemed strange. He felt uneasy every time she looked at him.

But throughout their flight, throughout this exodus, no one had looked at him or after him more than Maria. If it had made him uneasy, having her there had also made the time pass more quickly, made the hardships seem easier to contend with. He did not feel alone with her there, and now he remembered a saying of his father's: Only a stone can stay alone.

28

Maria was his companion—a mascot that seemed to bring him luck in these hectic days.

To Maria, David became a new type of image. The decent kind, whom a girl need not be frightened of. He looked pleasant and harmless to her. During their long hours of walking, Maria thought often of herself and of David.

What is happening to me?—she thought. Why am I changing, and what does David have to do with it? He looks like an ordinary boy, or is he? Boys have always known me as Shy Maria. To David, I am simply Maria.

She had not told David of her past, her home-life; she told no one about that. Even her friends would misunderstand, and would laugh and tease her.

David seemed so different, so mature. Maybe she could trust him with her story.

But, no, she would not tell him. What good would it do. It would harm more than help.

Her thoughts were interrupted by a command from an army sergeant.

"Piasecki," the sergeant said, "we must keep your people in line better. This is a war zone, and we can't let people straggle on the road like tired cattle."

"You are now two miles from the nearest town, and I will give you directions. There you will be registered and distributed to proper locations."

Distributed! All would have to do something useful here. For David, the army probably. For Maria, nursing or something else where she could help. Almost certainly, Maria felt, their separation was near.

As people began to ready themselves to march again, David looked around for someone to help. He picked up bundles for women, helped a man find the cane he had just misplaced. By the time David took his place, he was in the last row of the column.

Maria fell in alongside him.

"I guess we are first—from the end," he said to her.

"You have a good sense of humor," she said. "Where did you get it, David?"

"I inherited it."

"From whom?—your family?"

"No," David said, "from my people, from the Jewish people. My father told me that a sense of humor is, and has been, our greatest weapon, and so often our only weapon. It has helped us overcome persecutions throughout history."

"I've noticed this before," Maria said. "I had heard that Jews were different, but I never got to know one until the war started and I met you. I learned a lot yesterday just watching you and others. You seem to have a way of easing the tension. Where did you learn this?"

"From life. Being a minority, we aren't always able to fight persecution, so we have learned to laugh it off."

"How smart!" Maria said, "I wish I knew how to do it. You know, David. I heard only bad things about Jews, and now I can say it isn't so."

"You mean you have seen Jews and they are without horns?"

"No," she smiled, a little embarrassed. "I don't exactly know, but there is something different about you Jewish boys. You are more versatile and yes—that's what it is— your minds seem to work a little faster. I think you are practical in life; you find more than one alternative in anything."

She stopped a moment. Then she asked, "Why are Jews so clannish?"

"Well," David said, "if you're not accepted by some, it is only natural to turn to others, to those who want you."

"Is it possible, David, that I lived in a different world because the people I met didn't want me? Just until a few days ago I didn't realize that I'm capable of mingling with people . . . what a difference these days have made!"

"I remember," David said. "You were telling me that you were afraid of boys. Are they so terrible?"

"No. Not if they are like you."

"Oh, Maria, now you make me blush. There are plenty like me and many who are better."

"I presume there are," she said, "but I didn't meet them. The kind I knew considered me odd, strange—repulsive."

"Were you?"

"I guess I was."

"Why? What made you run from boys?"

She didn't answer right away. This, now, was what she wanted to tell him, yet didn't want to tell him.

Then it came out.

"Because of my mother's past."

"Did she have an illegitimate child?"

"Worse. She was syphilitic."

"What has that to do with you?"

"A lot, David. I lived in the same house. I had to face her every morning, at the dinner table, before going to bed. I couldn't kiss her."

She almost sobbed, now that she had told him.

"Why are you confiding this to me?" David asked.

"Maybe because you are the first one I've met who would understand."

"Do you feel better now?"

"Yes," she whispered.

"Then you shouldn't feel sorry," David said. "As long as life goes on, there are problems. As my father used to say, there is no way to escape problems. It is how we handle them that makes or breaks our lives."

Maria looked at David, but said nothing. He seemed ten feet tall to her now. She could not tell him that. She could not say anything.

She stopped alongside David as he picked up a tired little girl and put her on his shoulders. Maria took the child's hand, then made funny faces at her. Soon the child—all of them—were smiling, and none noticed how long the road was.

Then someone spotted the town, and a shout went up.

Before long, Piasecki had led them into town and to a school where an official welcomed them to Russia, and told them to assemble in a park where townspeople would come to take them to their homes.

6

THE REFUGEES, numb from their walk, sank down alongside their bundles in the park. They wanted food—a solid meal. But they had learned in these two days to wait, to take whatever they found. And what they found in the park was a moment's rest, and it satisfied them.

Soon the people from the town and the countryside began to arrive at the park, on foot and on horse and buggy.

Most of them were women—young and old, some with children, some without. The striking thing was that there were so few men, and what men there were squinted at the sun with old eyes, walked with the faltering feet of the old. The male youth of the village seemed to have disappeared.

The women descended on the refugees. They wore *babushkas* and heavy jackets, and there was the color of the farm in their cheeks. The Russian lieutenant in charge wanted the refugees all to line up, and the villagers to line up, too. But the women villagers would not wait. They descended on the refugees without waiting, choosing this one or that one for themselves.

"You two boys," a husky middle-aged woman said to two teen-agers. "Come to my house. There I have two daughters your age."

"Hey, good-looking," a red-cheeked girl said to another boy, who sat alone with his bundle. "Come with me. There is plenty of room. Only me and my baby."

An older, grey-mustached man with a hint of dignity asked a family of four to his house. "My three sons are in the army. There is lots of room and plenty to eat."

An old woman said to a girl, "Come on, daughter, with me. I'll show you my garden. We'll pick out the best fruits, fresh vegetables."

There was a place for everybody.

Maria and two other girls were picked by a hunchbacked woman. Maria ran over to David and said, "So long. Maybe I'll see you again!" Before she boarded the wagon Maria turned back and waved. She saw a young woman bending down to get David's little bundle, as if she was trying to assure herself that no one else could beat her out of the catch.

"My name is Natasha. What's your name?"—the young woman asked, looking straight into David's eyes.

"David."

"Come with me, David. I have a cow, two pigs. Just you and me."

David watched Maria and the other two girls as their hostess struggled over to her seat, a small narrow board right behind the horse's tail. The woman pulled the reins, made a strange noise with her tongue sucking through her teeth, and the horse, with his tail swishing at his mistress, moved into a trot.

David watched until Natasha said, "C'mon. What are you looking for? Let's go. Ten minutes and we'll be home. How long have you been on the go?"

"About two days," said David.

"I'll milk out fresh milk for you. Do you like goat's milk? I have a goat, too."

"Thanks, it really makes no difference."

"Oh, it will make a difference. You'll feel like new."

They were riding along the October Revolution Street.

"Before all the boys and men, from thirteen to fifty years old were evacuated, this was a paradise," Natasha said.

33

Now the little city of 12,000 looked deserted, with just a few curious passersby looking over the guests and hosts. The townspeople, unaware of the oncoming onslaught of the Nazis, looked more concerned about the fate of the newcomers than their own. Two women walked out of a store, stopped, and just looked, wondering what was going on. An old farmer, shoeing his horse, asked, "How far are the Germans?"

"I wish I knew," replied David.

The small city, with few men, looked like a ghost town.

"It isn't far anymore, maybe another ten minutes," Natasha said as if it was just a cat's jump. "You see this lumber yard to the right? My father was the manager, and my two brothers were working there. Yesterday all three were drafted and left me all alone. I've taken over one of my brother's jobs."

"Isn't it hard work for a girl?"

"No, all I do is deliver those boards to the electric machine, and my aunt cuts them. I lost my mother two years ago. Where is your family, David?"

"I don't know. It's a long story. Looks like your home must not be far from here." He tried to change the subject.

"Yes, not far at all. You see the hill, right behind it there is a small river. As soon as we cross the bridge we turn around a couple of streets, we walk through the market, then comes Lenin Square, an open field, a few more streets and we'll be right there." David took another breath and braced himself for another half hour.

"There is our market. Yesterday we had a busy day. Many women in this town and surrounding villages were saying good-by to their husbands, sons, and fathers. I was here yesterday all day watching women sob. War is terrible."

David looked around the market grounds. Bits of straw and newspapers were being blown by the wind all over the place.

"In normal times, all this was cleaned up as soon as market day was over," Natasha said. "Yesterday, almost every woman was too upset to do the sweeping. Hundreds

34

of men gathered near this statue of Lenin. Women hugged them, girls cried. Then the men were loaded on trucks. It looked like the whole population ran after them and shouted: 'So long. . . . See you soon.' It is so empty without them."

The place looked deserted and depressed. Not one soul. A few crows cruising around the stalls. On one of the stands, a cat was chewing on a fishhead. A rat showed up from under a wooden fruit box and a dog was barking at him. The heavy odor added to the sadness.

In the middle of the market stood a full-size statue of Lenin raised on a massive base. Twice life size, the statue looked heavy and could be seen for miles.

A large fence at the market exit was partially covered with a white poster and the large red letters screamed out: "Down with Nazi Imperialism." A second poster read: "We'll not allow the German dogs to rummage through our blooming Soviet gardens."

"Now," Natasha said, "we are going to approach a river. It divides the city from my village."

At the narrow bank, an aged man was fishing.

"Good afternoon, Sergei Semionovitch." Natasha shouted to him. He turned around, looked up, squinted and replied, "Greetings, Natasha." He continued looking, wondering who this stranger was.

A sudden explosion erupted far away. From up the narrow bridge they looked at the quiet rift of the floating water. It looked so peaceful, as if there was no war. On the other side there was a lone soldier standing guard. His rifle had the bayonet unsheathed. He watched them pass by. One could read in his eyes: "What a girl! I wish some of this man's luck would rub off on me."

"There it is," Natasha said, pointing her finger.

Just a few hundred feet were dividing them from her house. It was the size of a two-car garage, surrounded on three sides by beds of colorful flowers. She pushed open the unlocked, squeaky door, and David followed her a few steps in the dark.

She opened another door and light broke in. Between the

35

two doors was a goat, a pig, and a cow with her tail swinging toward the door as if to say: Welcome, it's this way.

Natasha paid them no attention.

"Here we are," she said, putting David's bundle down on a bench. "Come with me to the well."

She grabbed a pail.

"We'll draw water . . . wash up and eat." Back through the dark vestibule they went, into the freshness of the clean air, permeated by an aroma from the flowers and hay. Such peace! A narrow winding path, bordered on both sides with high, wild grass, led them onto the village's water source. Stones dry from the field, dirt mixed with clay, served as the base and frame for the well. Two wooden bars stemming from the base supported the winch and a heavy braided rope. Natasha turned the crank several times, and the rope plummeted to the bottom.

David stuck his head under the winch. The pail turned on its side, twisted, and then scooped into the water.

"It feels so cool and refreshing," said David, and his voice echoed more than once.

Natasha took hold of the crank and said: "Give me a hand." The two wound their arms in a circular motion and soon the pail appeared.

"Hold it," said David. "Let me take it off the hook." With both hands he pulled the pail down. Noticing the strain on his face, she said, "I can tell you are a city boy."

He carried it for a while. As he was trying to switch the pail of water to the other hand, she came from behind to join him. They smiled to each other as their hands touched on the thin wire handle.

"Around here we don't turn on faucets to get water," she said. "Here we have to work for it. My grandmother used to be very economical. With one pail of water she used to wash the dishes, the floor, and make soup," Natasha said with a laugh.

"Now leave the pail outside." She brought out a bar of soap, a cup and towel from the house. "There is soap, and I'll pour the water over you." She poured some on his head.

"Oh, that feels good," said David. He returned the courtesy. They dried on a stiff linen towel and walked inside.

"Give me that pail that hangs on that hook, I'm goin' to get you some fresh milk."

She picked up a milk stool, settled under the cow, and said to the animal, "Spottie, now be good. I have a guest in the house. Let's see what you can do for him." A couple dozen squeezes on the udder, and there was enough to go with a good meal.

With one spread of a newspaper the table was covered, and a few dozen flies were chased at the same time.

Natasha pulled up a rough wooden bench, and got out a pumpernickel loaf from under a cloth. A plate with cucumbers and tomatoes followed. No knife, no fork, she broke the loaf and put the chunks on a plate. David took a piece of bread in one hand, a cucumber in the other, then a tomato, and he downed them with a mugful of milk.

"How is it David?"

"Wow, it tastes better than manna from heaven."

"Have you ever been there?"

He laughed. "No, and I am in no hurry to get there."

Natasha exploded with laughter. "Hey, you know what? If you want to see heaven on earth let's go to the beacon light at the river."

They left the plate and their two mugs on the table and rushed toward the door.

"Wait a minute," said Natasha. "Let's take along some cookies and hard candy. Maybe you need an overcoat, David, it gets cold in the evening."

"No, I'll be all right"—he said hesitantly. She went behind a curtained partition anyway and returned with a black coat. "Here, this will fit you just right. Get your hands in. Right. Now you really look like one of our people," she said while buttoning the big, shiny, silver-grey buttons.

With Natasha such a good talker and David a good listener, the short walk to the riverbank passed without a dull moment. The pyramid-shaped post with a light on top brightened up the dim area.

"There is our pride, the river Markarovka. Every Sun-

37

day hundreds of couples sailed here. Today we can only look at it and reminisce."

A half dozen men were hastily working on a raft. They lined up logs one way and criss-crossed them with others. They were pounding long nails into them, and when they were finally linked together they pushed the contraption away from the bank, jumped on, and began steering toward the middle.

The boatman settled on their craft as soon as it floated. One rubbed a stone against an iron pipe which held a piece of cotton. Soon sparks appeared. A piece of paper, a few straws, a few pieces of wood—and a fire came to life. A pot of potatoes was placed over the fire. The men rubbed their hands and held them up to the fire. Someone started to sing; the others joined in.

It was the Volga song. Although far away from the Volga, their spirit was there.

In two voices they sang:

Volga, Volga, our Mother . . .
Let's pole it once . . . and once again . . .

The lyrics and melody echoed the rugged life of honest, simple people born on a river; loving that river; spending their lives working their blistered hands into callouses, their love for the water keeping them on Mother Volga for weeks at a time.

In summertime, their bodies baked brown in the sun, wrinkled from facing the sun. Pouches under their eyes, and sleepless nights, made each of them look years older.

David and Natasha listened. There was no need for any interpretation of the song. Each felt it in his own heart.

As the men floated away, their fire became smaller and the voices softer.

The songs of the raftsmen had not yet ended when several female voices filled the air from the opposite side. Three teen-age girls were approaching in a canoe. One was playing the mandolin, the other two were singing and rowing.

38

They sang loud and beautifully. In typical Russian harmony, they cried out about the rough life of wartime:

A Mother walked her boy,
For induction to the battlefront.
She cried with bitter tears:
Don't cry Mom, please don't.
Don't worry, don't fear;
Soon we'll defeat the enemy
And I'll return home.

Before they disappeared into the dark of the evening, the words of another song echoed. Their voices trembled as they sang, "So long, beloved town."

They sang loud, yet their loved ones couldn't hear them. "By now the boys are miles and miles away, maybe singing songs about their girl friends," Natasha said, very quietly.

The river Volga is called Mother because it is said, throughout history, when her enemies tried to defeat her, the Volga, like a Mother, threw up a defense for Russia.

The current carries the barges and rafts downstream; and to get heavily laden boats upstream was quite a problem. Yet it was done. Dedicated laborers, called *Burlaki*, slowly walked along the bank of the river towing heavy barges at the end of long ropes. Caravans of men spent their lives on the river in this way. It took more than muscles. It took heart and dedication.

In cold, rain, or scorching sun the *Burlaki* walked and sang. Russians believe that song tends to make hard work easier. Those who became exhausted often fell to the ground. They caught their breath, dipped their heads into the river, and went on with their work with a song on their lips until their destination was reached. When their job was done, smiles reappeared. A herring, a chunk of black bread and a potato satisfied their hunger and their aching bodies. A few crude tobacco leaves were wrapped in a newspaper swatch and a match was struck. One match served them all. After a few puffs, relief came. Talk commenced, and aching muscles and tired minds relaxed.

39

Always someone had an accordion across his knees.

One could close his eyes and feel the hardship; yet hear the music bring a fresh stream of life into the veins.

The stomp of feet is heard. The steps look simple, yet it takes skill and speed.

Several join in a circle, lock hands across each other's arms, and start to hop and sing. They jump up and down to the rhythm of the music. When one dancer gets tired another steps into the circle and carries on.

One suddenly wonders how men are able to pit themselves against the toughest of weather and physical challenge, for small financial reward, yet be so cheerful. What is the secret? What does it take for a man to be able to laugh from the depths of his being? There is an answer!

To them, tomorrow is another day.

They don't worry about how hard or how long they work. Hard work doesn't kill. And what is time, when one loves his work? They love to keep busy at sea from dawn to dark, facing the fresh wind. Then, after a hard day's work, when the sweat is wiped away, a good bite to eat and a joyful chat with friends completes the day. The *burlak* puts his burning feet into the refreshing Volga river, throws his line in, and catches fish to bring home for his family.

His wife knows that a man has to work hard for his family. The children know that Papa is somewhere at sea. They wait for him to come, and when he does they swarm all over him.

They don't look for goodies from him, they know he doesn't have any. When Papa arrives he brings them the one gift they want—himself.

He, too, is overjoyed to see them, touches them, talks and plays with them.

Mama gets busy cooking the fresh fish he brings home. The whole house is united and happy, chatting and laughing. The atmosphere is alive; they all create it themselves. The smell of fresh cooked fish already suggests a good tasty dinner. At the table Papa is most important. He sits at the head of the table. Then comes Mama sitting at his side and the rest of the household, all around.

Many poets have written beautiful poems about "Mother Volga." The "Song of the Volga Boatman," is a great favorite.

"When I was a little girl," Natasha said, "our school went by ship all along the Volga. It takes two weeks to get to the end of the river. David," she said, "you should have been here a month ago, when happiness was spinning in the air. All the accordions, guitars, songs and dances; for us it was a life without worry."

"I'm beginning to realize now how little happiness there is left. Come Sunday evening, I used to walk with my girl friends, arm in arm. Boys from surrounding villages pursued us. They tried to break us up. "Hey girls,' they said, 'you look like sisters.' And we in turn: 'Are you brothers?' We'd stop, chat, giggle, and before the evening was over the boys had their arms around the girls, and they were walking away in all directions."

Suddenly, Natasha said, "Let's go home." She put her arm around David's waist, put his arm over her shoulder and said: "This is how we walk around here."

David blushed. "I guess," he said, "girl and boy rules are international."

The moon disappeared far behind a mountain and a cool wind began to chase the dark clouds. Then came a thunder roll, then a few more.

"Let's run," said Natasha, "or we'll get wet like two alley cats." She broke away through a narrow field path. David kept right after her. He watched the side movements of her hips and her arms. Her long hair flapped across the shoulders of her yellow and orange flowered dress.

The rain started to come down. David took his coat off, and put it over their heads as an umbrella. The harder it came down the closer Natasha leaned her head toward David's.

"Here we are; home, sweet home," Natasha said, with relief. She opened a squeaky door and the animals greeted them with bleats, lows and grunts. She awarded a few of them a friendly tap or two as they walked inside the house.

Unable to see, she tapped her hands along a wooden shelf, looking for matches. A few strikes and a match lit up a candle.

"I have *golubtsy*, caviar, curded cows' milk or goats' milk, and a good-smelling black bread. What'll you have, David?"

"Just bread."

"How about goats' milk, David? It's good for you. One who drinks goats' milk a hundred years lives a long time."

Soon all sorts of greens were added and the newspaper over the table was almost covered from edge to edge.

"Eat, David, tomorrow you have to go on with your hard journey," Natasha said, much quieter.

"What are you going to do tomorrow?" asked David.

"To me tomorrow is just another day. On to my job, then back home alone like an orphan. Would you write a few words to me, David?"

"Yes, I will."

An old alarm clock was ticking away breaking the monotony of the silence. It was past midnight.

"What time do you have to get up to go to work?"

"About five. Maybe we'll call it a day. Let me make your bed." She spread papers on the floor; then she pulled out from a wall closet a perina, a heavy feather quilt, and spread it over the paper. She leveled the down evenly and put a large pillow against the wall.

"Would you like a candy to sweeten up your life, David?"

"No, thanks."

"Good night, then, David. Sleep well." She blew out the candle. David took his drenched shoes off. They felt like a ton. He put his shirt and pants on a chair he found nearby.

The squeaking floor and the sound of the old sofa springs gave away every move of Natasha's undressing. The fall of her shoe increased the beat of David's heart. Every move of her dress and her other clothing made his blood run faster through his veins.

The rain poured down. The little house shook with each

42

thunder. They could hear the sound of raindrops penetrating several spots of the room. Clip, clop, clap clip! "Oh, oh, oh, if we don't want the house floating away I had better find a couple of pails," Natasha said, walking around barefooted in her long flannel nightgown. In the shadows of a flickering candle, Natasha bent down, picking up a few large dishes and a pail and setting them under the falling drops.

"Sorry, David. Of all the nights, you had to pick a rainy one. Here we have a saying: Suffer Cossack and you'll become an Ottoman. Don't mind it, just close your eyes and you'll sleep like a baby. Now if I could only get my hair dry."

She reached for a towel and put the candle out. As tired as David was he couldn't fall asleep. Was he too tired? Or was it the presence of Natasha in the same room? He listened to the rain hitting the tin roof. It sounded like a heavy drum accompanied by lighter tapping on the inside. Like a disorganized orchestra, he thought. David lay on his back with his eyes wide open, seeing nothing in the total darkness. His mind was working too hard to sleep.

His thoughts were interrupted by Natasha.

"David, are you sleeping?"

"No."

"Your hair must be wet; you may catch a cold. Can I get you a towel to dry your hair?" Her approaching footsteps could be heard before he could even answer.

She went down on her knees and put a towel on his head, rubbing his hair gently.

"Thanks, Natasha—you are a wonderful hostess."

She straightened out his hair and combed it with her fingers. Both became silent. Never, since they had met, had there been such a long break in their conversation. David could hear her breathing. The sound of rain disappeared. They could only hear their heartbeats. A warm sweat covered David's forehead. He could feel her breathing becoming stronger.

Neither one felt like talking. It was a sweet moment for

43

both. A warm comforting feeling of not being alone; of two hearts at peace.

The stormy wind almost blew the roof off. But they did not notice.

The tip of her long hair lightly touched David's hair, then it brushed his neck. David felt her hand on his shoulder, then her cheek against his face. She pressed her chest against his outstretched arm and whispered in his ear.

"How was dinner, David?"

"Just wonderful, Natasha. Wonderful."

"David, you know what?"

"What, Natasha?"

"How would you like to have a little dessert?"

Both burst into laughter. He put one arm around her, then the other. She fitted into his arms as if she had been made for them. They locked in an embrace.

"David," she said. "What will you think of me?"

"I can't think."

"You may think that I'm an example of Russian free love. I never felt so free in my life with any boy."

"Nor am I a gigolo," David replied.

"I can tell that you are a gentleman. To think of it— a girl having to seduce a boy."

"You didn't, really. I could see it coming just seconds after you kneeled at my side and kept the towel over my head."

"Tomorrow you are leaving. I may never see you again. Perhaps you will remember me as a bad girl."

"Why should I? You did everything for a stranger that any human being could do. Is it your fault if you are a normal girl?"

"David, you are so understanding. I love you." She sealed his lips with a warm kiss. "You don't have to say anything, David, just hold me tight."

The clock was ticking away. The rain dripped into the dishes.

Somehow, they had rid themselves of the few things they wore, but they were not cold. Somehow, alone as they were, they were not alone. Songs were with them. And the people on the river. . . .

Later, still embracing, they fell asleep. Not alone. Not alone.

"David. Hey, David. It's eight o'clock."

"Eight o'clock? Natasha, you are late for work."

"I'm not late, just sick. Sick about you going away. My boss will understand. I never got sick like that before. A girl has the right to get sick once in her lifetime. We better get up now and eat."

David stretched out his long arms, yawned, and turned on his side facing the table. All the dishes on the floor were filled with rain water. But the dripping had stopped and the sun had begun to peek through the small windowpanes.

Natasha got busy preparing breakfast. A light smoke was coming from the mud oven. Quietly she hummed a song. She tried to stay happy, but the minutes were ticking away and she felt sadness creeping over her.

"What are you cooking so early in the morning, a whole dinner?"

"It's just a few cakes for you to take on your way."

"What for?"

"So you can think of me . . . at least when you eat the cake anyway."

"Just don't forget to give me your address, Natasha."

"Please, David, let's not talk about it yet."

She chanted a song:

You are going away,
Yet you'll be with me;
One can't order a heart.
Without parting,
There is no longing.

The clock's hands kept moving, hastening the time.

"It's almost time for us to go to the marketplace. It's 9 o'clock," remarked David.

"Yes, my baking is about ready." She wrapped it up

45

in newspaper, the only paper available in the house. "Here are two shirts, a coat, and a blanket for you, David. Nights in Russia are cold. It'll all come in handy."

"True, but I couldn't accept it," David said in a voice filled with emotion. "You don't have much yourself."

"Go on, foolish boy, I have a house, a job. . . ."

"I can't, Natasha. I just can't. I may not be able to repay you."

"Repay? I *want* you to have it. It'll make me feel good just knowing that you feel warm; just like I felt in your arms. I want to remember you being in good spirits, like the day we spent together, and not like just someone who owes me a shirt. If you ever give it back to me my joy in letting you have it will be taken away."

"You know, Natasha, whenever I shared a candy with a friend, my Grandmother called me a 'Russian soul.' Now I know what she meant by it. Now I realize how much more I have to go to deserve it."

"Oh, David, but you do deserve it. Just don't forget to drop me a line."

"What'll people say when they see me with such a big bundle?"

"Smile, David, and tell them you earned it. Let's go, you are asking too many questions."

She roped the bundle to his back, turned in front of him, held him with both hands and gave him a long kiss. As their lips separated, Natasha gave him one more hug and said: "That one is to keep you warm."

"And this one is for you, Natasha," said David, as he kissed her again.

The half-hour walk to the railway station went by fast, too fast for both of them, a walk full of joyful conversation. At the railway the refugees were already gathering. The hosts had come along.

"I guess," said David, "I'm not the only one who made friends."

A passenger train was waiting and ready for them.

"Where are we heading for now?" people asked. But

no one would say. "It's a military secret," they all said. Soon a loud call was heard: "All refugees aboard!"

People quickly shook hands with their hosts. Many were wrapped in hugs. Natasha began to squeeze David's arm. He turned around. Her eyes became glassy.

"Good-by, Natasha. Thank you again for everything. I won't forget."

"Only time will tell; I will see by your letters." He put his arm over her shoulder, turned and stepped up the steps. Both managed smiles.

Soon the train began to move. David leaned toward the window and saw Natasha waving her yellow kerchief. The train moved faster, and soon the sight of her smile and her wet eyes quickly faded.

7

THE TRAIN STOPPED at a weed-infested field with nothing in sight. The refugees called this place No Man's Land.

There were only two men waiting for the transport. One had three stars on his epaulets which identified him as a Senior Lieutenant. He was accompanied by a Sergeant. They surveyed every refugee from head to toe as he stepped from the train.

Their suspicious looks worried the people. What are they going to do with us?" they asked. "They can't shoot all of us. They aren't even armed."

"They certainly can't feed us here," complained a wiry-looking woman holding on to her two screaming children, their faces covered with dirt.

"Just look at the two of them. They look as if they haven't had a thing to eat themselves for the past week."

"All men from 18 to 45 line up!" ordered the Lieutenant, using his hands as a bullhorn. "Line up to my right."

"Now listen, men," continued the Lieutenant, "You are being drafted into the Red Army! Sergeant Forlov is going to lead you to the Induction Center."

Through fields and side roads, the men were marched to a temporary army camp.

"Shall we sing?" the sergeant asked the marching recruits. When no one responded he began the song which was the answer to Hitler's attempt to take the Russian capital:

Moskow mine
My loved one
You are undefeatable.

The recruits joined in singing the well-known song and the dull marching became more spirited.

David noticed the twelve gold buttons on the Sergeant's uniform and thought to himself:

"Soon I too will be wearing them. Who would ever have thought it possible?"

A product of a capitalistic system, David never thought that there would come a day when he would be fighting for a Communist system. In Poland the Communist Party was outlawed and its atheistic ideology was unpopular in the ghetto where religion was practically the only thing left for one to live by. But that's war—he thought. Why should he feel guilty about it? He didn't invite Hitler.

He thought of the letters he received from his aunt in America. If she could only send him a ticket so he might go to America. They were also fighting the Nazis; but the Americans were not to be seen. The Russians were. And they were deadly serious about fighting Nazism. David knew what he could expect under the Nazis and he decided that he would even join the devil, if necessary, if it took that to fight Hitler. Soon he learned more about the Russians.

For the first time in his life David got to share a dining room table and living quarters with non-Jews. Ever since he could remember he was always told not to play or even talk to Gentiles because they would beat him up! This frequently happened. But here he found older, more mature young folks, who never asked his religion. To atheists, Judaism or Christianity or any other religious belief was a poison, harmful to the working man. Questioning religious affiliation in Russia was embarrassing and unpopular. David saw no horns on any of them, nor could he see angels' wings attached to them. No nation should be characterized by generalities, but David did find some general characteristics about Russians in wartime. They were suspicious of foreigners. They seemed able to suffer hardship and hunger more than a westerner. They were, to a surprising extent, able to sing and dance and play a musical instrument.

David recalled the scene on the Volga River where Russian voices penetrated his heart. About Natasha? He wasn't sure whether he was in love with her. But to forget her warmth wasn't easy. During his off-hour David asked the Sergeant for a piece of writing paper.

"All of the writing paper goes to the front-line office," the Sergeant replied. "Tear off half a page from the newspaper. We have no ink here, but here is a "chemical pencil." Wet it on your tongue and write over the print. We also have no envelopes, no glue. When you are done writing let me show you how to fold it into a 'triangle sleeve.' Just write the army code unit, and no stamps are needed."

David sat on his bunk and began:

Dear Natasha:

Today, two days since we parted, I learned that I'm 175 miles from you. But it seems much closer.

Your warm breath keeps me warm and your words give me hope. The kind of hope that says, we'll soon defeat the enemy so we can be united with our loved ones.

If I ever survive this war in one piece I'll never complain for the rest of my life.

I thought I lost everything since I left my home and family, but today I found a little something. It's the pride of becoming a fighter against Nazism. I look at my green and black epaulets, and I see room there for my future officer's stars. It may sound like a silly ambition, but all my life I was pushed and shoved, undermined and belittled. Now I want to be someone who can discipline others and tell others what to do.

Don't worry Natasha, the two stars will not get in my
eyes. You are the only star that shines in them and
lights up my life.

There will come a time when I'll join the front-liners
to fight the German agressor. I'll be a full-fledged man
then. With a front pack on my back, a helmet on my
head, and a rifle in my hand; maybe cold and hungry,
yet I'll be ready to fight. I'll be a real man.

All this for sweet life . . . for our families, our people;
yes, for life . . . and how sweet it is.

I would like to survive this war just to see the defeat
of Nazi Germany, to see my family, to see you and the
beautiful world of peace and brotherhood in which it
will be worth living. And you know what else? I think
I really love you.

Your David.

The train carried David to an army camp where six
months later he was commissioned a lieutenant in the Red
Army. The train dropped Maria and the other girls at a
small city, where they understood they would be employed
as nurses and clerks.

David and Maria saw each other just once on the train,
just long enough to say good-bye.

He wrote a letter to Natasha, telling her all he saw from
the train's windows. How like her, he thought, to insist he
should write. He knew, as the Germans advanced, that
there was almost no chance that mail would get through—
and if it did get through, she might no longer be in her
home town. But she had insisted, so he wrote. She said she
would write him, although she had no idea where in all of
Russia he would be. If she could write, she said, so must he.

Now, in the uniform of a Russian officer, he was looking
out the windows of another train, and his thoughts were of
Natasha.

Upon graduation from officer's school, he was assigned
to travel to a Siberian labor camp to draft 320 men who
would form a unit under his command. His superior officer
had told him, "These men are not a good lot, lieutenant, or

51

they would not be in this camp. So be sure you choose them wisely. Your future depends on how they soldier."

The train's first stop was Kuibishev, a beehive of people moving in and out of the station. Judging by the nationalities and races he could see from the window, it was a real League of Nations.

There was one young Cossack who held his attention in particular. His chestful of medals flashed in the sun beneath a garden of ribbons. He wore his uniform with remarkable elegance. The jacket and his handsome body seemed to be made for each other. Green jockey-like pants neatly billowed out of his tall black boots. Boots of soft leather resembling an open accordion were fitted tightly to his knees. The four stars of a captain glittered from his flat epaulets, and the curls of his black hair were partially tucked into his *papacha*, his black fur hat which was embossed with a red star.

An army march filled the air, and the Cossack walked with his head up as if he were in a parade.

The stations were huge. Slow trains sidetracked to make way for trains of military importance. The passenger trains were all filled and the traffic was heavy. Militia and MPs checked documents. In one station, a train with iron bars over the windows and a guard of Russian soldiers drew everyone's attention.

This train carried German prisoners heading to the far rear of the fighting area. They munched on bread, or simply sat outside their train talking, while guards kept watch over them. They drew many taunts from the Russian travelers: "Hey, Fritz! Tell us Fritz. What happened to your blitz?" The Germans ignored it all, as if they heard nothing. At one point they were ordered up, to exercise their legs. The Russians were big on exercising.

Hundreds of civilians were herded into another group of boxcars, guarded by another group of armed men. They were Soviet Germans from the Kishbishev area on the Volga. When the Nazis tried to cut off the Volga at Stalingrad between Archangelsk and Kuibishev, the Russians had decided, for security reasons, to evacuate the citizens of German origin to Siberia. They sat on small bundles and spoke quietly in a German dialect.

Finally, after sitting an hour in this one station, David's train moved off. Again the woods closed in. Streams mirrored the white of the clouds and the fresh blue of the sky. Then suddenly would come a cluster of wooden buildings and lonesome grey houses that looked as if they grew out of the ground.

Occasionally, women were seen in felt boots and grey, dirty work pants, making repairs on the track. They looked big and masculine. Their oversized work clothes made even the thin ones look fat. With all men from eighteen to fifty away in the army, it was not uncommon to see women taking over the back-breaking jobs. There is no weaker sex in Russia. Women are equal in Russia, so the work is equal. And some of them, David thought, could outwork any man.

The train approached Sverdlovsk, a city of about a million. In the station, surrounded by a web of railway tracks and passenger overpasses, David felt like he was sitting in a huge outdoor train factory.

He felt a hand on his shoulders. It was a Russian he had met earlier in the journey.

"See," the Russian said, "I told you Sverdlovsk is fascinating. I wish I could show you some of the gold areas. There is no other country on the globe with such an abundance of mineral riches."

The Russian's love of his country was obvious. He was proud of all its accomplishments, and he showed it when he said, "The price may be high, but it is worth it."

David asked, "What about all the sacrifices; the frostbite, the malaria people get from the mosquitoes?"

"When you think you are building a paradise for your children," the Russian answered, "then nothing is too hard and everything pays off. No man lives for himself. He is born to pave the way for others: the new people, the young people."

The Russian boasted about the hardships.

"Hard work doesn't kill anyone," he told David, "but idleness does."

A few days later they arrived at the Pacific, at the port of Vladivostok. White houses mingled with trees were scattered over a hill which sloped toward the sea. Busy like bees, the cranes rattled, loading and unloading ships. The green-blue waters were rich in fish, seals, and whales. The air over the city smelled like the sea and the fish.

Winding streets led David and the others from the port uphill to the army command unit. There were soldiers all over, all of them armed, for Vladivostock was an important fortress and naval base. Batteries of mighty guns, underground hangars for planes, heavy concrete fortifications and pillboxes were placed all around the city. They were smartly hidden and camouflaged. Only flowers and woods could be seen from a distance.

David reported his arrival and presented his papers.

"You are going to take a train to New Siberia," the commander said. "There you will see Mayor Kospak and present this envelope."

A mile walk through the city took David back to the station where he boarded another train. There was a corridor on one side and sleeping compartments on the other. A porter walked toward him, carrying a large tray. David bought caviar and a glass of steaming tea.

The bed in his sleeping compartment was hard, but what right does a soldier have to look for comfort during a war? If only he is alive, he is doing well.

For four days the train steamed through the woods. The Siberian forests are the largest in the world, with desolate open spaces and swamps running wild and untouched.

The railroad looked like a thin corridor cutting through endless wilderness. Occasionally the train passed a small community. Then the great forest closed in again, and there was nothing but a wall of tree trunks on both sides of the tracks.

"This is called the Taiga," a greying man said to David. The man was in his fifties, dressed in a skin coat with a *papacha*, a fur hat, pulled half over his ears.

"Thousands of square miles are impassable swamps. They are treacherous because a man sees nothing under his feet, but the moment he steps in it, he sinks up to his neck in the soft, cold ground. Unless a friend is nearby, nothing can save him. The swamp sucks him in.

"And the mosquitoes—they attack men and drive them insane."

"On windy days, the Taiga roars like the surf of the ocean. No man can live alone there."

The Russian told David that he lived outside a Siberian city with a population of less than 100,000, and that he was a trapper. For his job, he said, there was no better place in all the Soviet Union. Bear, wolf, raccoon, mink, boar, fox, all abounded, he said. And there were birds, he said, that had never seen men.

From time to time, in the darkness that had fallen, flickering lights from huts showed in the train window.

"You'll see communities only along the railroad," the Russian said. "But when we have won the war and the young men return, we'll make a heaven out of this whole area for millions of people. It's going to be our America of the future."

"If the blitzkrieg keeps up, we'll trick the Germans into these swamps. Part of them will sink in the quicksand and the rest will be eaten up by mosquitoes."

In the morning there was more activity outside the train. Women with white kerchiefs tied around their heads drove tractors or walked behind horse-drawn plows.

"You are approaching the Urals," the Russian told David. "They divide the European and Asian parts of Russia."

Now different faces appeared outside the window. Faces with an Asiatic look.

Georgians, with fur caps framed with wide cloaks of natural black sheep wool, were known as horsemen. These mountaineers still carry daggers stuck in their belts. They hardly use them, but it is a part of the traditional dress to which they cling. Their wives still wear their traditional wide and long bloomers, tied around the ankles. The women can always be recognized by these clothes and by their colorful silks and rayons. Their heads were mostly covered, and they looked like walking parachutes.

Here David must alight and pick the men that were to make up his troops.

At the edge of the station pavement, a Uzbeck sat cross-legged, in front of him a large white handkerchief holding a wide, flat bread and a mixture of vegetables. This custom was imported from Uzbeckistan, a Soviet Republic bordering Afghanistan. These Moslem people sit on their legs in a criss-cross position for hours. David tried it for just a few minutes, but the pinchy feeling sent him right back to his feet.

The Uzbeck tore the bread into shreds, and guided one little piece after another into his mouth which was covered by long, uncombed hair hanging down from his mustache and his goat's beard. In the palm of one hand he had a cup of tea, the color of black beer; and he sipped it after every few chews.

Several white towels were wrapped around his head. He seldom turned his head although his slanting eyes observed the world passing by. His teacup was small, so he kept filling it from a teakettle, directing it up and down, up and down. This movement is supposed to give it an extra stir and a little extra flavor.

A military station wagon took David to a labor camp called the Correctional Institution. Criminal and political prisoners were sent there, and they worked in coal mines or chopped away the enormous trees, building roads.

After a brief check of identification papers by the guard at the gate, David was led inside. There was one shaky table with a couple of old chairs, and a shelf made out of cracked boards. Papers were all over. The damp smell was more than enough to give one a headache.

"I'm having the prisoners line up for an interview," said an Elder dressed in a sloppy *kufaika,* a short quilted coat tied with a thick belt hitched up with a large star-shaped buckle of tarnished brass. "You may choose from them."

The men were ordered to come in one at a time. Disheveled and unshaven, they walked in with a look of curiosity and bewilderment. They asked: "Is it an amnesty? Are

56

we pitched into the army or what? Hey, anything would be an improvement. . . ."

". . . Who knows maybe the Lord will overhear our pleas."

After name, address, age and nationality, the main question followed: "What are you in for and how long?"

"For hooliganism—but comrade I was drunk, and when you are drunk. . . ."

"No explanations are needed, the lieutenant is not the judge . . . ," interrupted his superior. "Next!"

"How did you get in here?"

"For vagrancy—Comrade Lieutenant, I got to drinking alcohol and didn't show up for work for a month. My foreman at the airplane factory in Tbilisi called me a parasite. The next thing I was sentenced to one year and sent out here. Please take me into the army. I want to fight for my country. . . ."

"Okay, that'll be enough. Next."

A middle-aged man came in with a slick look in his eyes. "When the Germans besieged Stalingrad an order came out to turn in every ounce of steel so it could be melted into arms. I found an old bedrail in my attic. I sold it on the black market for five miserly rubles, and got caught. Now, all this for one lousy, rusty piece of junk. Please give me a chance, Lieutenant, please."

"Next."

"What's a handsome man like you doing here?"

"I'm a tailor by trade. I worked in the textile factory. One day I was caught walking out dressed in two suits."

"You stole a suit and put it on yourself?"

"Yes, comrade, but everyone else does it. Didn't you hear the saying that the Soviet Union is the richest country in the world—everybody steals and there is still enough left for such a great army?"

"It isn't funny," his superior cut in. "The lieutenant isn't laughing. Can't you see? Go back to your work."

The next was a tall, broad-shouldered man. "It happened last year in October. I was working in a Kolkhoz, a communal farm as a tractorist. Farmers dug out the svekla, the sweet potatoes, and lined them up for burial before the cruel Russian winter arrived. When they left I took some and buried them in a secret place."

"Why would you do it? It belonged to you, too. You could have eaten till your stomach burst. Greed, ha?"

"So I made a mistake. Look, comrade, I'm not doing any good here. In two days I can learn to drive a tank and help fight our common enemy."

David liked the word "common enemy." The prisoner sensed it. He left the room hopeful.

David chose young men from all walks of life. Nazasov—a college boy from the Republic of Turkmenistan. He got his wish by saying, "I'm here for raping a girl. Where I'm volunteering for, there won't be girls; boys I don't bother."

A Russian civil-sailor from near Leningrad said: "I got drunk and five militia grabbed me and tried to subdue me. Then three more came. I fought all eight off single-handedly. Can you imagine what I can do to the Germans when I'm sober?"

Anatoli Golkin made his questioners laugh when he said: "I swiped two brassiere straps from a factory. I needed them like a hole in the head. There are things a man learns the hard way. I must have been crazy. Those who are really crazy don't even know it. That's the trouble with them. I know I'm crazy that's why I'm not." He got everyone good and confused, but he got his wish at the same time.

After the selections were made the men were lined up. A dozen buses waited for them to take them to the nearest bania, a public bath. A platoon of girls in their early twenties were already there waiting for them. With men up to the age of fifty in the armed forces, the girls were made to do barbering.

The men were ordered to get fully undressed and the girls got to work. In just a few minutes their hair was shaved. It wasn't a neat clipping but the hair was gone and that is all that mattered to the sanitary unit of the army. That was a new experience to the men. Remarks flew all over.

"Well, an order is an order. . . . What are you going to

58

do after my bottom clipping? . . . Sorry, I never took my pants off in front of a lady. . . . Oh, c'mon, I'm not a lady, I'm the barber, besides what do you think, I never saw a nude man? . . . I got no time, sit down and I'll give you a clipping so you can get under the showers.

A caravan of *tzeplushki* were reserved for the new draftees at the Vladivostock depot. These were ordinary boxcars with old, cracked little iron ovens to keep them warm.

For a while, everything was orderly until the bread came. One loaf for every six men. As soon as it was brought out they pounced on the portions like vultures, each one trying to get a piece that seemed a little bigger. The biggest fight raged over the crust, the *okrajczik*. Foul language rang all the way into David's quarters in the neighboring boxcar. Curses flew in all directions.

At the first station, David entered the noisy boxcar. They stopped talking, several got up.

"Sit down," ordered David. "Your dialogue is unbecoming soldiers of the Red Army, and your profanity is inexcusable. I heard you insulting a comrade over a crumb. How petty can you get?"

"Rapuchin, I'm appointing you in charge of this group. You are going to be responsible for your men. You are required to report to me on those who don't get along. I can still send them back to where I picked them from."

The pardoned prisoners were attached to a labor battalion near the front. Their function was to dig trenches for mobile radio and telegraph units. The work was backbreaking at times, but the men didn't complain as long as their stomachs were full. They found conditions on the front line more favorable than in prison. David had been the right person to select the men. But to deal with them day in and day out was a different matter.

Kind and gentle, he found himself in a new world. The men constantly argued, swore and made noise enough for thousands.

"Please boys," David pleaded with them, "can't you

59

talk softer?" His pleas at times were unanswered. Even the quiet ones used to flare up like a match.

Winter arrived, and along with it a merciless frost with swishing winds that carried snow from all over. The early winter of 1942 caught David and his people in their summer clothes.

They had arrived at the end of September near Stalingrad. An early, rugged winter found them in lightweight uniforms consisting of an undershirt, a thin army shirt, jodhpurs, leggings and shoes.

An order from the staff came to dig a *Ziemlanka,* an underground quarter. Equipped with dull shovels, the men couldn't even scrape the surface.

Daily, layers of new snow froze over the hard ground. Heavy snowflakes fell and a cold drizzle turned it all into a sea of ice.

David radioed the staff for winter clothes and food. Everything was paralyzed. He saw his men shivering, jumping, trying to warm up their feet. Some rubbed their red ears. His tough men from the Siberian woods hardly complained, while he almost froze inside.

"Hello," David radioed on the Morse key, "this is unit 614. My men are freezing. It's impossible to do anything without winter clothing. Without food for the last twenty-four hours, over."

"Unit 614, this is Krasnoe Solntze calling. Take the men into the nearest village and station them in farmers' homes. Then contact us for further orders."

David quickly ordered his men to get their shovels and line up for a march. Sliding over the icy snow and trudging knee-deep through the snow, they came to a village.

The number of men per house depended on the size of the farmer's home and family. Soon they were all distributed. David picked the home of an old woman who seemed to be kind.

"Come in, lieutenant," she said. "I'll heat up for you a pail of water, give you soap, then I'll fix you a nice evening meal. Then, there is next door a young woman. You know what I mean."

"No, thanks. The hot water and the meal will do."

"Ay, I see you are a good boy. There aren't many who go to sleep alone in this village. The damned war has made every woman sex-crazy. With the men gone they don't leave the soldiers alone.

"Imagine what'll happen when the poor men return? My own daughter falls in love with a new soldier every week. What's going to happen to this madness? How are they going to explain their new babies? It's becoming so prevalent, that a woman who stays away from men is considered not well.

"They all say it openly. A woman is human. She needs love. With this war love flew out of the window, so people are hanging on to sex; the little part that is left of it.

"First, the girls preferred to remain somewhat modest, so they were shy on the first evening. The soldiers got angry and got their way. Soon the girls declined to resist. They said, if you can't fight them, join them.

"It's only a year since the war started, and look what's happening. They sneak out to a barn, right next to the animals, or they order grandma to take the kiddies out of the house to a neighbor. When soldiers are stationed in this village I wouldn't dare to walk in on any of my neighbors, day or evening.

"Stay out *mamasha*, they tell me—I'll call you when I need you. What a world! We have here a woman in her sixties, but she's still got some juice left in her. One day a soldier who stayed over wanted to kiss her goodnight. He was young enough to be her grandson and she felt somewhat embarrassed, so she said, 'young fellow, why would you want to kiss an old lady with one tooth in her mouth?' 'One tooth, one kiss,' he said. When the young soldier went to retire into another room, she had the audacity to wake him up. 'Hey, young man, look here. I have another tooth.' "

"Well," said David to himself half jokingly. "If she only had all her teeth, can you imagine all the fun she could have had?"

A buzz of the radio awakened him.

David rushed to the receiver. "This is Krasnoe Solntze. What transportation is available in your village? Over—"

"—614. There is one frozen Kolkhoz truck."

"A helicopter will arrive soon with more instructions."

Soon it landed, just a short distance from the house in which David waited.

The helicopter was equipped with a well-furnished office. David smoothed out the wrinkles of his uniform and hurried up the two steps into the mobile staff headquarters.

Inside, his chief, Colonel Nasimov, sat at his desk with gobs of papers piled up in front of him. With his eyes turned on David, the chief looked serious, concerned and slightly pale.

"Lieutenant," he said, "I was just informed by wire that the Germans surged forward at several of the front sections, cutting off our food supply. Due to the character of our work, we must stay on here until a number of units evacuate."

"I'll order the truck to be at your disposal. Pick a driver and four men for loading and leave at once for the following destination. Here we are now," and he pointed a finger at a wide map.

David—tired, and still unsure of the terrain—listened as the officer, using his finger as a pointer, gave him directions. He was to take his truck and several men to another point to get food.

The officer's finger raced over unmarked roads and across what seemed to be nothing but fields. David asked him to repeat the route several times.

After he had saluted and left the helicopter, he still was unsure where he must go.

But he ordered four of his men into the truck and hopped in himself next to the driver.

"Turn toward that bunch of trees along the river," he said unrolling his own map. "We are going for a short ride to get food for our unit."

8

THE ROADS THE COLONEL had pointed out were not roads at all, and soon David and his men were lost. The wrecked plane that was to have been their most important landmark was not there, and the name of the Russian village they were looking for had been somehow mispronounced by the colonel.

The simple trip became a nightmare.

Russian peasants on the road simply raised their eyebrows and shrugged when David mentioned the name of the village. They had never heard of it.

But David knew he had to find it. It was a must, because hundreds of troops, unfed for two days, depended on it for food.

David and the driver were in the cab. The four men on the open platform behind them clung to the stakes of the truck to keep from being blown away. David's agony was intense. He feared that if he failed, the future would bring him a military sentence, a dishonorable discharge, years in a work camp. Maybe even death.

But the feeling that tormented him most was the danger of his unit weakening and falling into the hands of the Germans. Who knows? By now, maybe he and his five men were already encircled by the Germans. In modern war, no one can really tell until one actually sees the troops facing him.

"All right, Kulakin," David said. "Let's pull up at the first house we see, before we get blown into hell by these winds."

A few raps at the door brought forth a scared voice: "Who's there?"

"We are from the Red Army."

"Come in, boys. Thank God, I thought the Germans were here. You must be cold and hungry. Sit down. I'll fix you something to eat."

David unfolded the map, pulled his flashlight out and with hands shaking from the cold, he tried to read.

"Eat boys," their hostess said. "Eat to your best health. Whenever I see our boys around, I think of our men. Maybe someday they'll surprise us and come home."

"*Babushka*, Grandma," David asked, "tell us, have you heard of a village, Mihajlovskoe?"

"Mihajlovskoe? Mihajlovskoe? Let's see. . . . Is it supposed to be near here? No. There is no such village, and I have lived here for my whole sixty-eight years."

"What are we going to do?" David asked his men, who looked at him despairingly.

When there was no answer, David said, "Well, thanks, *babushka*. We just have to get moving. We must push on until we get a clue and find that place. Oh, how I wish that colonel of ours was here to show us the place he said was so simple and easy to locate."

"Good luck, boys," the old woman called after them. "Good luck. God bless you."

"Let's go comrades," David said. "We have no time to spare. The only thing left for us is to look and look until we find that magic spot."

"But, lieutenant, it's pitch dark. With no lights, how are we going to make it?"

"Get on that platform and start the motor, Kulakin. One meter an hour is better than staying put. If we can't drive through that snow we are going to walk through it.

64

If we begin to think less of ourselves, and more of the boys back there, we may not find it so hard."

The motor started, and they left. The truck bobbed and weaved over the ruts.

They could see nothing, but what else could they do?

David hoped they wouldn't wind up back at their own unit without finding food. He could imagine the sarcastic colonel greeting him: "Oh, good evening lieutenant. Did you have a nice trip? I don't see any food in your truck. Did you at least pick up a few dead Germans?"

Kulakin broke in. "Where in the world are we going, lieutenant?"

"I am only one, and you are four," David replied. "Can't you put your heads together and come up with a good suggestion? No carlights, no street signs, just a bunch of local farmers who don't know either. What can we do, but keep moving until we are lucky?"

"You are right, lieutenant," said one of the crew. "There! There is something that looks like a house. Let's stop and ask there."

"Hey," David exclaimed. "You are right. But it looks to me like a barn. Maybe, since the people don't know the village, we should ask the animals. But wait. There is a light. Maybe someone is there feeding his flock."

A young man in his twenties was emptying a bushel of corn for squealing pigs. David became uneasy. Men of his age should be in the service. Why was he still home?

"Tell us, young man," David asked firmly, "where is the village of Mihajlovskoe?"

The young man let out the rough, ugly sound of a mute. His face showed remorse because he could not answer.

"Mi-ha-jlo-vskoe?" David repeated loudly.

Limping on one foot and dragging the other, the young man got down on his knees, wiped the straw clear of the grounds, and motioned for David to write the name in the earth.

He looked at David's writing, then raised his head toward the barn roof, as if trying to find the answer there. His face relaxed then, and he smiled.

65

He took up a stick and wrote "Michailovka."

Then he walked outside into the snow and pointed toward the road. He grabbed David by his sleeve and pulled him back into the barn, where he scratched out on the ground "one kilometer on the road."

David shook the young man's hand warmly, and the young man blushed. They could say nothing more. But it did not matter.

Back in the truck, David said to his comrades, "I hope this will be our lucky road." The driver answered, "We will know in less than half an hour."

The truck rolled and slid through the snow, and at one bad place slid and didn't stop until it was in a ditch. Out they all piled to push, while Kulakin rocked the vehicle back and forth. Nothing worked.

"Okay," David said, "we are all going into the woods for branches and bushes. If we put them under the wheels, maybe we can get out."

They brought back branches, then they pushed again.

"I wonder," said David, "if Columbus worked this hard when he discovered America."

"Of course not," Kulakin replied. "He was smart. He went by boat."

They laughed and pushed again, and finally the truck lifted itself from the ditch. They climbed back in. But they had only rolled a few hundred yards when a great roar under the truck sent them flying. A plastic bomb, planted on the road by the Germans, blew the truck almost apart. For a moment, after the bomb, there was total silence. Then they heard the moaning. Kulakin, lying across the seat of the cab, was hurt in the stomach.

As they all rushed toward him, they saw a half frozen beagle jump into the cab. Wet and shivering, he found warmth alongside the wounded man. Kulakin held his bleeding body.

"I can't stand it!" he screamed. "Help me!"

"Take it easy, Kulakin," David said softly. "You will be all right. Try to hang on. One man will stay with you, and we will hurry to the village for help."

66

"Hurry," the driver said. "Hurry."

David and three of the privates began to run in the direction of the village, but soon their legs gave out on the cruel road. They dragged their feet like old men. Soon the wind and the wet snow shut out the cries from behind them, and the howls of the beagle.

The distance to the village seemed to grow with every step. When they finally came to a house, David dragged himself to the door and rapped.

"Who is there?" a heavy voice answered.

"Red Army men. Open the door."

The wrinkled face of an old man, holding a lit candle, showed itself at the door.

"What brings you here on such a devil's night?" he asked. "Come in."

"Tell us, *Papasha*, is this Michailovka?"

"Yes. Who do you want?"

"Tell us where the military unit is."

"This," the old man hesitated. "I cannot tell you this."

"Oh yes you will," said David fiercely, pulling his revolver.

The old man said, "Lieutenant, I am a Soviet citizen like you, and I cannot tell you military placements. Your papers, first."

David was embarrassed. He put his revolver away and fumbled in his wet pocket. "Here," he told the old man. "And I am sorry to have treated you that way."

The old man looked at the papers, then said, "The army is in the hills at the other end of the village. It will not take you long. But first, let me get you a drink of water, or food."

"There is no time," David told him. "We must go."

Outside, powered by new hope and new strength, David and his men covered the distance to the army camp in a few minutes. Soon, they met the sentries who took them to the staff office.

An officer said, "Your papers indicate you should have a truck. Where is it?"

"It hit a mine. My driver lies inside seriously wounded."

The officer, a Major, picked up a telephone receiver and without hesitation dispatched a medical unit. Then the Major arranged for a new truck, with food for David's men.

As David was about to leave, the Major said, "Lieutenant, have you had any rest?"

"Rest?" answered David, "If I don't get going now I won't be able to rest until the end of my life."

David got behind the food truck, and they followed in the direction that the ambulance had gone. The ambulance crew removed Kulakin. He said good-bye to his fellows with a weak wave of the hand.

David hoisted the puppy into his truck, and the men named him Dushka, which is Russian for Little Soul.

David was wary of enemy presence all through that area. He watched carefully as he drove, and ordered his men to do likewise.

It only took them minutes to find Germans.

The Nazis had spotted them and set up an ambush. They waited for the truck to come closer. A shot from a German light cannon set the truck on fire.

David, with Dushka in his arms, jumped for cover. The dog escaped and hurried across a field. The soldier next to David in the cab was wounded. He managed to open the door and fall out, but the flames from the underside of the truck engulfed him.

A jagged chunk of metal had cut David deeply on one leg, and a bullet pierced his arm. But he got to the other side of the truck where the Germans could not see and, in spite of his leg wound, ran across the road and dropped behind a thick bush. Then he all but crawled inside the bush to hide himself. It worked. Through an opening, David watched as the Germans moved in on the truck, firing until they were sure all were dead.

All that food, David thought. His comrades dead. His unit starving somewhere, waiting for this food. All for nothing. His throat was dry and he was bleeding. But he could not move until the Germans were well away. He

68

played dead. Had the Germans suspected otherwise, they would have finished him off.

He was both a Red officer and a Jew, and that meant a double death. He had heard stories of how the Germans made prisoners undress. They knew the Jews were the only ones who were circumcized. On top of that, he was wounded. The Germans would not have wasted time taking a wounded man prisoner. He would be shot.

He resolved to wait until dark, then try to find the home of a farmer.

How far he might have to search, he did not know. How would he get there with his leg? No answer came to him. But unconsciousness did.

When he awoke it was night, and there was no sign of the Germans. He was stiff from his sleep in the cold, but he forced himself to move. He would have to crawl. His left leg, badly wounded, would not support him. And his right arm, broken by the bullet, pained him incessantly.

It took all he had, to crawl even a few feet. But the alternative was death. He would fight while he could!

David crawled along the side of the road, inching along until he reached a high point and could see a sleepy village. There were occasional cannon shots. But they were far away. The moon forced itself upon the night like the beam of a giant projector. David lay there a moment. He took out a photograph of his family. Then he looked up and said out loud, "God Almighty, I heard, many times about the miracles you have done. Wouldn't you please save one for me? I want so much to see all the people in this picture again."

He put the photo back into his wallet, feeling a little embarrassed. He had never talked to God before. He had hardly ever worshipped him, even as a boy.

He turned back on his stomach and began to crawl again. It seemed to be within his reach, maybe several thousand crawls. Through his mind ran the words of his Russian commander in officer's school. "The fight against Nazism will be to our last breath."

69

Whenever his breath seemed about to run out, David rested.

And, now, he heard a dog bark. The dog smelled him and came closer, then ran away. Then it came back. The barks awakened a farmhand who came from a house David had not seen. He held a pitchfork in his hands.

"Please," David said, "help me into your house. I can't stand up."

The farmer was dressed in long underwear and high boots. His wife, who had come out behind him, was draped in a blanket. They bent down to take a better look at David.

"My God," the farmer said, "look at his pants, his jacket, all covered with blood. Let's pick up that poor lamb and take him inside."

"Be careful," David said. "One of you take me by my good right foot and the other by my left arm and try to pull me. Now. . . ."

The pain made David black out.

When he awakened, he was in the farmhouse and a small girl was crying.

"She is an orphan," the farmer said. "We took her in from a neighboring village." He turned to the girl and said, "Don't cry, baby. We are going to take care of him real good."

David asked them to bring him cold water, towels, sheets, and scissors. He drank straight out of the pail as if his stomach had no bottom to it.

"Pull off my boots," he asked the farmer, "and hand me the scissors."

He tried to cut his pants off so he could get to the wound, but the blood had dried and his pants were glued to it. He poured water on the wound until the blood loosened.

The wound bled openly. Thin towels were almost immediately soaked.

"How long since you were wounded?" the farmer asked.

"I have lost track of the time," David said. "It was yesterday morning, I think."

"That's a long time."

70

David poured water on the wound until it was clean. Then he and the farmer tied it with heavy towels.

When he had been bandaged, the farmer's wife brought him tea with vodka, and he fell into a deep sleep.

Then there was a pulling at his pillow.

"Wake up," the farmer said, "troops are coming."

"Ours?" David asked.

"I don't know. It's dark outside."

"Help me to the window," David said.

Tanks were moving along the road, and David squinted to make them out.

"If they are Germans," he said to himself, "then goodbye. Might as well shoot myself before they do."

Then the strains of music came faintly from the road. Russian music. The soldiers atop the tanks were singing.

"They are ours," David exclaimed. "Ours!"

David found new strength. He hopped outside, dancing a cripple's jig, while the farmer ran, waving his arms, to the road. Now David could see the Red Star on the tanks, and the uniforms of the men.

The farmer returned with a Russian captain. David identified himself and asked to be taken to the rear hospital.

"I cannot," the captain said. "We are heading toward the front lines. But I will have our medical unit look at you before we go on."

Red Cross jeeps and a bus loaded with nurses stopped.

A nurse checked David's bandage, gave him pills to ward off infection, and instructed him to have someone from the village drive him to Lesniki, in the other direction, to the field hospital.

The farmer nodded. "I know Lesniki," he told David. "I will see you there."

He turned, put his hands to his mouth, and hollered in the direction of another farmhouse. "Sergei! Sergei Ivanovich! Get your horses and buggy. We must take this wounded lieutenant to Lesniki."

The reply came.

"Ladna! Ladna! Right away."

At Lesniki, David's bandages were changed and he was

71

put aboard a train for a regular hospital in Tashkent, capital of the Uzbek Soviet Socialist Republic of Russia. It was the largest city in Soviet Asia, and a long way from the front.

One morning, during his regular visit, the head of the hospital, Dr. Ephraim Markman, asked David, "Where are you from, lieutenant?"

"From Vilnius."

"Vilnius. Vilnius. . . . Where did I hear that? Ah! Just a few days ago a man arrived here. . . . Let me look him up."

The doctor pulled a registration book from his pocket, studied it, and said, "Ah! Here. A man of your city. Room 407. Israel Berger."

"Israel Berger!" David shouted. "But he is my closest boyhood friend. Can I go to him now?"

"Take it easy," the doctor said. "That is a floor below. I will ask a nurse to take you in a wheelchair."

Outside room 407, David could hear Berger talking to a nurse. David could scarcely recognize the voice. It was even more difficult to recognize Berger when David looked at him. His head, neck and chin were heavily bandaged, and the small part of his face that showed was bronze.

David wheeled himself to the bed and said, "Israel!"

Israel looked up and the white of his eyes doubled as he exclaimed, "Oh no! David! To meet you here. You are alive. Alive."

For a while they sat staring at each other, hands clasped, unable to speak.

"What a small world," Israel said with an excited voice. The two began to reminisce about their loved ones, families, friends. They hadn't felt so close to home since they parted from their city of Vilnius.

"As I left town I saw your grandfather, Chaim," said Israel. "He stood at his doorstep watching me hurrying off with a few bundles. He waved to me and said, 'I wish I had your legs, Israel, and I would follow you. Good Luck!' On my way home from school I used to stop at his window, where he had two large glass jars filled with water. Inside

72

there were bloodsuckers. I used to watch those creatures with a sour face. I always wanted to ask, was he a doctor?"

"He was a *feldsher*," David said. "You may call it sort of an 'underdoctor.' My grandfather thought of his bloodsuckers as a wonderful contribution to human well-being."

"How did he treat his patients?" Israel asked curiously.

"Well, my grandpa would take a patient into his office which consisted of two chairs and a table in his bedroom. He would lay the patient on his own bed on the stomach, and pull up his shirt. Without blinking an eye, he would scoop the bloodsuckers up and over the patient's back."

"Wow, I feel the creeps going over my body just by listening to it," said Israel.

David went on.

"He was the only one in my family who wore a *yarmulka*, a skull cap, at all times. He was an honest and God-fearing man. On the High Holidays he joined the family in our synagogue. It was called the Old-New Shul because of a paint job put on the outside for the first time in about a hundred years.

"Inside we had to split up. Women and men were seated on separate sides. In accordance with the orthodox religion, my mother and sister were jammed into a segregated narrow strip. There was room for twenty chairs, but somehow close to a hundred managed to be pressed in.

"They were cut off from the men by a few boards and towels, some clean, some dirty; even remnants of old aprons and patched up dresses were hung over a pole or laundry cords.

"All this to block the view of the men. The young girls used to peek out to try to see their fathers and brothers, but the elders had their heads and minds in the *siddur*, the prayer book, where it belonged. As my father explained to me: 'When you go to pray, you go to pray. Not to look at girls.'

"The men's section used to be crowded to capacity. If you had money, you sat; and if you didn't, you stood up. But everybody had the right to be seen and heard by God.

"With that sticky crowd inside I wondered whether God

73

himself could see everybody; but when it came to hearing them, there was no doubt in my mind.

"The people made so much noise, they could wake up a dead one. When the moment came that the worshippers asked the Lord for a good, prosperous, and healthy year, the air was filled with an explosion of voices. Men shook forwards and backwards, then switched sideways; pleading and shouting so the good Lord could hear them.

"The women's hearts mellowed and tears fell on their clothing, the prayer book, on the floor. Old women who cried the hardest would wipe their nose with their fingers and cry some more. When the benediction was over the women's section was so wet that the moisture helped the breathing in the men's section.

"On Yom Kippur I always had a headache and was near fainting towards the end of the service, in spite of my unsuspected reinforcement with a half loaf of bread.

"I once asked Grandpa what kept those people on their feet for twenty-four hours without a crumb of food or a drop of water. 'Spirit, dedication,' he said. 'You think everybody is an ignoramus, an *am hooretz* like you?'

"The day-long service used to wear me out," David said. "I tried to sneak out, but Grandpa always caught me by my arm and caged me between him and my father—with Grandpa holding me by my sleeve and my father holding me by my pants. I had no way of getting out. I had to come up with a white lie like 'I'm sick!' Getting to go out was a real treat. It was like coming from an old tired world into a new one with plenty of fresh air.

"On the top of the steps leading into the place of worship, there always were a few self-chosen speakers. Nine times out of ten, the subject was Palestine. Their main argument was how to get rid of the British and create a Jewish state. The moderates spoke in favor of immigration. They claimed that Palestine needed more Jews to overcome the Arab majority.

"The rightists were less patient. 'We have waited for two thousand years for our Promised Land,' they said, 'and if I listen to you I'll wait another two thousand. Why wait?

We should get hold of guns and ship the British back to England where they belong. They have their dominions, colonies and "shmolonies" all over the world. Aren't we entitled to a little piece of our own land?'

"At times two or three got up on the same narrow upper step, arguing and shoving. Once, the door opened from the inside and the two speakers were pushed accidentally down the steps. But they didn't give up. They moved up the steps again and started to address the listeners, both at the same time.

"The audience got so confused, it didn't know to whom to listen. Should they go to Palestine and wait forever until the British decide to leave them alone; or should they start a population explosion on their own to outnumber the Arabs?

" 'You can't do it' one exclaimed. 'An Arab has several wives. The women do all the dirty work while he plays checkers. So he has all his time and stamina. Several days after one of his wives has a baby she goes back to work, while he rests in bed and accepts the congratulations for a job well done.'

" 'We Jews have to work for a living,' he argued. 'How can you expect a Jew to think of a population explosion after he returns from a hard day's work? The Arab has it so much easier. He gets up in the morning, pulls the sheet from his bed and he is all dressed. A Jew needs a pair of pants, a suit, a shirt, a pair of shoes. . . .'

"On a Moslem holiday, Arab women go to the sacred river, and so as not to make it a total loss, she washes out all her sheets.

"A Jewish woman has to go to a *mikvah*, a spiritual bath where water is above her knees and no lifeguard is on duty.

"Or take the Arab man, another voice continued. They have got it much easier. When they walk into their mosques they take their shoes off and make themselves comfortable praying to Allah resting in a sitting position.

"Come the High Holidays, on Yom Kippur we have to stand most of the time on our feet and with an empty stomach to boot.

"How can we outrace the Arabs in babies?" said the rightist. "What we need is to go to Palestine and tell the British to go home."

"And what if they decide not to listen to you?"

"Then," replied the rightist, "we'll have to send over the Zionists."

This was their way to air their frustrations, caused by the prejudice of the non-Jewish world. In essence, they were an insecure people trying to find a solution to their shortcomings, each one, in his own way.

For hours David and Israel went on like this, their stories and their minds far away from the war that had brought them together again like this in so strange a place.

Later, when he had returned to his own room, David lay for a long time, looking at the ceiling, recounting all the stories again to himself.

9

WHAT DAVID DID not know was that at precisely that same moment, his brother Aaron lay on his back in a partisan camp not too many miles from Wilno wondering about David.

Aaron, too, had tried to run ahead of the Nazis that day in Wilno. But the parachutes David had seen had encircled him and, like so many other refugees, he could run no more.

"Where do we go from here?" people asked frantically. "Those are Germans!"

German parachutists appeared behind trees and bushes. With automatics in their hands, they came out from several directions.

"Halt! Hands up!" came a booming command from a bull-horn.

"All this night—for nothing," someone said.

"That's it. This is our end," an older man said.

"Alle Zurück! Everybody back to your homes!" another command came.

No one tried to resist. There was no way to break away from the powerful Germans. It was certainly suicide to try. People just gazed at the well-dressed, clean-cut Wehrmacht men. For the time being it was hard to believe that these well-groomed people were capable of the atrocities they eventually did to the German Jews.

The people walked back hoping. "Maybe? Who knows?" asked one woman. "Maybe they are not as bad. You know the newspapers don't always tell it as it is. With God's help we may fall into the hands of nice Germans and they won't harm us."

Such hopes didn't last long. Soon all sorts of orders began to scream at them from posters plastered all over the city. Jews are not permitted to do this and that. . . . Jews are not permitted to be here and there. . . . Jews must report by such a day at such an hour. . . .

After every order there was a firm warning: "Jews disobeying these orders will be shot."

This constant threat of getting shot began to sound like an endless refrain. Aaron, along with thousands of other Jews were herded into stuffy ghettos, and when they became over-crowded, the Germans found their own simple solution. Since Germans considered it uncivilized for people to live in overcrowded conditions, they shot them.

People tried to obey their orders; buy favors. But no matter what they did, they could not buy compassion. There were no good Germans to be found. All followed the pattern of their Fuhrer and Fatherland.

Those Jews who had preferred to see the Russians leave were ready to have them back. But that was just wishful thinking. The Nazis were everywhere in Vilnius and it looked as if they were there to stay.

The word equality became alien to the Jews. All their lives they were not given much of a choice, and now they had no chance! It was not a matter of rights, it was only a matter of surviving. Hard earned Jewish money gradually became so many pieces of paper. It could hardly buy anything. Suddenly, all Jews, regardless of their cultural or financial standing fell to the lowest depths of degradation. Professor Movshovitz dug an outside toilet alongside Piper the Swiper; and Sobol, the prominent attorney, cleaned the smelly kitchen ward along with Bentske, the notorious masher. Yankelevicz, the big department store owner, shared a haystack with the pimp, Yoyne Rasputin.

Alongside was Bunimovitz, the founder of the Buminovitz bank, one of the few Yiddish banks in the world. He was considered to be the only millionaire in Vilnius. There were stubborn rumors that he was worth at least five thousand dollars and maybe as much as eight! In the ghetto he shared one pot with a notorious beggar. Reb Gotenhiml, a religious zealot, found himself sharing crowded living quarters with Apikojres, a shady, shabby character who got enjoyment out of coming to synagogue early on Yom Kippur, the Day of Atonement, to stand in front of the entrance eating a roll to spite the worshippers.

Members of political rival movements became virtually united into one state of misery. Former members of the Bund who advocated progress among the working class under the discriminating system in pre-war Poland, realized that they had failed. The left-wingers from the *Hashomer Hatzair*, whose aim was immigration to Palestine and pioneering the future of the Jewish State, realized that their dream was far from coming true. The Betarists, the school youth from Masada, the legionnaires and other conservative Zionist movements who advocated all kinds of political moves, ranging to armed resistance were there too. They no longer had on their colorful uniforms, and their pride and courage had begun to fail.

All political factions found themselves intimidated. Suddenly, all their differences became irrelevant.

From history they learned that the existence of their people was an endless chain of suffering and reprisals. But, somehow, through a stubborn desire to live, and through an occasional miracle delivered by God, the chosen people emerged over the ruins and rose over the dead to new heights, which brought them back into a flourishing cultural and material existence.

They could look back at their own past. All their lives they had suffered from anti-Semitism under the Czar, the Poles and the Lithuanians. Some were arrested by the Soviets, and all of them dehumanized by the Germans.

In the meantime, the same Red Army who claimed to be the liberator fought for its own life, trying to escape the Germans' deadly onslaught; and the Americans were too busy with the Japanese.

Vilnius, so remote, far away and strategically so unimportant, became, to the allies almost a forgotten place. True, the ninety thousand suffering souls from Vilnius were a reality, but there were millions of others in the same position and there was no way to save them—at that time, anyway.

Over a period of many long days and nights Aaron told his pal Boruch how the Nazi nightmare came to be real.

Just think of all the philosophers who have gloried in the twentieth century; the poets whose beautiful words have been inscribed on endless pages; the immortal musicians, who have tried by way of sound to bring forth the wonders of the beautiful life and world in which we live; the religious leadership, which so strongly believed that the good Lord takes care of the sick, the poor, the unfortunate; and all the statesmen and politicians who promised a heaven on this earth.

The world could boast of many brilliant minds. But all together, they managed to overlook one small item: A party of a dozen beer drinkers who met in a Munich bar, and there formed a Nazi movement!

While Hitler marched forward and grabbed the countries he wanted, the politicians were waiting. A staunch anti-Communist, Hitler would probably strike at Red Russia. Then, who knows? Maybe he will go too far, and there will be two dead birds with one stone. So the talk went.

People used to say: While the western politicians buried their heads in the sand, the Nazis began to bloom.

And many Jews, exposed to pogroms for so many generations, accepted it as a part of life.

The defeatist slogans went on: "It isn't easy to be a Jew, one has to pay the price for being one." "Persecution will follow us no matter where we live." Pushed around, abused, and spat upon, they became accustomed to accepting humiliation, and to swallowing their pride.

Orthodox Jewry continued to see its fate as a punishment from God. They were told that the reason the German Jews suffered persecution was because they were becoming so assimilated that God had to bring a Hitler to remind them who they were. Some wondered why God, whom we loved and worshipped, permitted so many innocent people to suffer so much pain. But for that some had other answers too: "One for all. . . . All for one. . . . We must pray harder for those who are straying from the Jewish faith. . . ." But others asked: "Why doesn't He punish those of other religions for neglecting Him?"

Is it more of a crime to break away from Judaism than from other faiths? So why do those who rob, beat, and murder, remain unpunished? On the contrary, it was the worst of the criminals who held the reins of power, whipping the pious, the innocent, the women, even the children. . . .

The Nazi onslaught was regarded by many Jews as a carbon copy of the pogroms of the past—just another Haman. This time it was Hitler. He was, perhaps a little worse, but the Jews had survived Haman, and they hoped to outlive Hitler. Few saw special reason for greater fear. Jews had suffered throughout their existence, and this time, they thought, it was just another chapter in their struggle to survive; another chapter of history.

The bitter taste of the Nazi dogma wasn't strange to the Jews. Their leaders, including some of the flamboyant pre-war elders who spoke up on their behalf in front of the not too friendly Polish government, became less and less influential under the Germans.

Most continued on with their new masters. Although their intentions were good, their efforts to coexist with Nazism failed. They fell into the same trap of the Nazi death machinery, with many of them crushed to death along with their co-religionists.

"Let's hope our shrewd leaders will outdo the Nazis," people said.

"Where can we run? The Germans are all over."

To most there was no other alternative than to sit put and wait for something to happen. But what? In peacetime, Jewish immigration to Palestine was prevented. Those who didn't have relatives abroad interested in getting them out, just sat around hoping for better times.

They prayed: "Next year in Jerusalem," but they remained at home. They said, "If I forget you Jerusalem, forget me." They never forgot Jerusalem; but they were unable to forget that the Jewish man had a moral responsibility to provide for and feed his family. But he could still hope—"next year in Jerusalem."

Even *Di Shtarke*, The Toughmen, as the underworld was called, became soft, weak and cowardly. In the first few days, before the law was posted all over the city boards, threatening death for black-marketeering, the Toughmen did everything from peddling a watch to exchanging Polish zlotys for German marks.

These ruffians, who just days ago had controlled the economic power of the city and manipulated many politicians, were, like the rest, scared by the harsh law. Never afraid of a fight, they found their alibi: "Things are still not so bad yet. We are not permitted to buy in stores, go to movies . . . , but look how many more things there are left for us. We can trade and still make a living."

The same tough scum who were capable of attacking anyone, froze at the sight of a German. All their lives they hadn't put in an honest day's work, and lived by sponging off others. They were convinced that they could do the same now. In the ghetto there was always a sucker to be found.

To those shady characters, the over-crowded surroundings, the smelly air at night and the dog-eat-dog hustle were part of their life. With time to spare, they "fixed" decks of cards, invited the "rich ones" to play, and cleaned them out. They used their talent at fraud and theft in the ghetto where a piece of bread could make the difference between life and death. A few reformed, and became helping hands to others. They were known to belong to the group of "either-or" characters. Either they hated you, or they loved you. There was no in-between; and whichever way they felt, they practiced it to an extreme.

In the meantime, people began to find out that Jews were being taken out to be shot. Their hearts were heavy but still hopeful. Their answer to it was: "They will kill some, but they can't kill us all." They waited for the worst to pass. "It'll have to pass, because it can't go on and on," others speculated. The Germans soon learned that the easiest way to destroy the Jews would be by eliminating resistance.

Knowing that Jews throughout the ages had been wary of foreign rulers, the Germans decided to let them have their own rulers. To some Jews this was a hopeful sign. Jewish self-government!

The *Judenrat*, taking to their task with serious intentions, soon learned that they were only tools meant to execute orders from their German masters.

Many, instead of inspiring their youth to take to the forest and join the underground, helped to enforce the rule of the Nazis. Some knowingly helped supply the German master with groups of Jews to be sent off for elimination. They lived under the illusion that by so doing they were permitting others to survive. But in time they found out that the survival was only temporary. Some committed suicide, rather than go on with this bloody game.

Yet, there was no spontaneous wave of revolt. Most Jews just succumbed and cooperated with the authorities. Occasionally, a partisan would sneak into the ghetto and urge young men to leave with them. But they were scared. They demanded a guarantee that they would be safely delivered to the partisan camp. And who could offer such a guarantee?

Some young people dared to stand up to the Nazi master. A young man who refused to answer one of the SS abusers was slapped in the face twice on both cheeks. When he spat in the Nazi's face, the dumbfounded SS man pulled his revolver and pumped five bullets into him.

Two other men who refused to cooperate made a daring escape. Several hours later they were surrounded, roughed-up, and brought back handcuffed.

Death lay on their faces. With their heads down they were led at gun-point back to the camp and into the box. It looked like a coffin standing up. Under strict security measures, they were guarded by the two SS. With no food, no water, the doomed men stood up the whole night through. The next day something was added—a scaffold.

All prisoners were ordered to witness the event. The doors of the torture boxes were opened and the two escapees staggered out. One of them stumbled and fell on one knee but struggled back to his feet. As they were led toward the scaffold they straightened themselves up. They were brave, and tried to look that way before their fellow inmates. They stepped up on the stools.

As the hangman reached for the ropes, they shouted with all their might: "Down with Nazism! Long live freedom!" Soon they were dangling in pain from the ropes with their faces turning from red to blue.

People turned their heads away in disgust. Women sobbed, children cried, men coughed in an attempt to keep from choking. An older man said in Hebrew: *Yisgadal veyiskadash.* People listened until he finished, and then said "Amen."

Some knew the two boys personally, others just by sight. Suddenly, they became closer to all.

"Fine boys," a woman whispered, "their only crime was that they wanted to live like the good Lord meant them to live."

The people walked to their barracks. Some couldn't swallow the small portion of bread given them for breakfast.

Regardless of frost or burning heat, prisoners stood for roll call at dawn. If the count didn't come out right they had to stand for two or three hours more. Then they marched to work for hours. Their feet were wrapped in rags or were bare in wooden clogs. They worked for twelve-hour periods in the stone quarry or gravel pit.

For breakfast they got a low-grade coffee and no bread. After a long day of work they received soup and bread. That took care of twenty-four hours.

Every day inmates passed out, and the Germans were right there to finish them off as if this was what they were waiting for.

84

As hopes became dimmer, people became more frantic. "What can we do?" the elders were asked.

The answer was: "What will happen to all of our people will happen to you . . . , so don't run. You may get the SS angry and they will let it out on all of us."

All were asked that resistance should not go so far as to endanger other lives. What they couldn't see was that without resistance their lives were hopeless. Most put their faith entirely in God's hands, which was not enough. Religious leaders were simply too frightened to spell out the fact that God helps those who help themselves.

In the beginning, when people still had a few posessions hidden, they offered it to their guards, trying to get a favor. When they became possessionless they still tried to prolong their lives by blind obedience.

Those with imagination wormed their way into becoming repair craftsmen. They continued talking themselves out of one death into another, until their turn came. Aaron saw them falling like flies. He sensed the SS pattern of total annihilation. To avoid mass resistance, they executed their program of annihilation gradually. Slowly but surely.

In small groups some were trapped into digging their own graves. As long as there was one breath left, the people were gullible. An inmate wouldn't give up hope, even if it meant that he was the only one to survive. Most had no other choice but to leave their fate to the hands of the ruthless exterminator.

Every day Aaron could see the systematic elimination of the inmates. Always were they conscious of the iron SS discipline. One could get shot on the spot for not tipping his hat before an SS man . . . for falling behind . . . for getting sick, exhausted . . . for not answering Herr . . . for a thousand other "reasons." The SS was the law!

People saw their relatives and friends shot down every day, and they hoped maybe, God willing, it wouldn't happen to them. To the SS their lives were cheap, worth nothing. In some cases it wasn't even worth a bullet. Some did their job of killing by injecting disinfectant into hearts, others by making people stand in freezing water, still others operated the poison gas. They used a club, a bottle or whatever implement they could get hold of. An SS trampled a young boy to death because he overslept. The same human monster put a cane at the throat of a snoring man, stepped on both ends and strangled him. "There was one good thing about death," Aaron thought, "if I die I won't see all this anymore."

The cells were overcrowded, the sanitary conditions were bestial. People whose resistance had sunk to the lowest point died first.

The camp authorities made a practice of using prisoners of suitable mentality to act as their assistants. These were made block prefects, named *Capos,* and enjoyed considerable privileges: more food, no backbreaking work, and some power. At a time when everybody was laid low, to those few, it still felt good to be a bit privileged. That false feeling of importance led some to drastic action. They forgot who they themselves were—ordinary prisoners whose life was only being extended until they finished their jobs of preparing others for their doom.

Burda was one of them. Power went to his head. One day he clubbed one ward to death. He stopped at nothing to make an impression, just to please his Nazi attendants.

The Nazi hate propaganda pushed people to animal-like behavior. They were called *Chapunes* or Grabbers. Twisted by the venom of hate, there were those who volunteered to grab a Jew and deliver him to his oppressor for ten rubles.

"I have an order to send away an unproductive element, that is, young children and old people . . . but let's see, how much money do you have?" Volodia asked a man whom he suspected of having some money left.

The desperate one turned to Volodia, the greedy *capo* who made them believe that he had some power which might save them from execution. He was known to many as the good looking kid, with a bright smile and dark hair brushed from his forehead, up and down to his neck. He was remembered as the same youngster who changed parties, like gloves, jumping from one political organization to another depending on what party uniform looked best on him.

"Please, Volodia," some pleaded, "save my mom and dad, I'll pay whatever you ask."

"Three hundred marks," he called out coldly.

"Here is one hundred marks, that's all I have." He counted it twice and stacked it all away into his pocket along with a thick bundle of money and said: "Well, maybe I can try to find a substitute."

"Must you?"

"Must I? Are you joshing? The Nazis want a hundred people and you know how the Germans are. It's not ninety-eight or ninety-nine, but a round hundred. If I don't supply this number, they'll take me along and shoot me instead."

The ugly war has turned a few individuals into animals. Volodia had been a soft-spoken human being in peacetime. In camp, when his stomach began to complain of cramps, he soon learned to be otherwise.

For a few extra crumbs he even learned to mistreat friends who had been kind to him.

The well-groomed young man with that million dollar smile turned into a shabby dog with a nasty growl. There was one thing about him that didn't change. He had always been one who wanted to be on top, more important, to have more money. Rumors about prospective shootings brought inmates to him with mercy pleas. "Please, Volodia, I have an old mother, save her. . . . I have a young boy, save him, he is only twelve, send away to death an old one, instead . . . save me, I'll give you my gold watch . . . we have good money stacked away, you can have it, if you save us."

For money he played with lives. He took money even when he knew he couldn't help. The Nazis used him all the way. With their mouths they approved of his work, but with their eyes they saw a traitor, one whom they would like to destroy.

Nobody likes a traitor, and so Volodia went on from one day to another piling up ransom; and then when all his pockets bulged, the SS shot him, like a dog infested with rabies.

The Nazis were "building a better world" over the bodies of women and children. A better world for themselves and no world at all for others. They never asked themselves how good a world can be when people shoot their way into someone else's home, rob them of their belongings, slaughter their livestock, eat their food, drink their wine, and leave their children hungry and thirsty, facing death.

This living death began to affect the minds of the survivors. Men digging graves for the executed could see themselves buried in them. Motl, the baker, whispered a prayer, then asked a friend to push him into the grave. They knew he meant it, but no one took him seriously.

His body shivered, his hands trembled: "Please, fellow Jews, I can't make myself do it. Just one push, a little poke will do it. Please. I can't stand to see all this or live through it."

His outburst lowered their sagging morale to a still more alarming depth. This routine of dying had become, with the inmates, part of an existence. The question in their tired minds was not how they would die, but when. They could see it every minute. They could watch their own funerals, something they never dreamed they would ever live to see.

In a world where fields and waters are sufficient to feed everyone, they faced death from starvation.

In a world with so much space, there was no room for them—only a pit into which to be squeezed, like sardines piled one on top of another; body piled on body.

Stripped of hope, people went about as if they no longer cared what would happen to them.

This was the moment in their lives when they didn't have to worry about how to die, but how to live. Their doubts that such life was worth living grew from day to day. Among the condemned was Doctor Pinchus. He was born in Lipuvka, a poor section of Vilnius, where he lived among his patients. There lived the poor, the feeble, the unfortunate. Pinchus had been raised with them and called them "my people." He had always worked hard, helping his father to save some money for his own education.

He never left his people. "I could never abandon them," he said. "They are part of me. If I leave, who is going to take care of them?"

Only few had money to pay him, but Doctor Pinchus served them all equally. He wore his shoes out on the streets covered by rough-cut stones and loose planks with protruding nails. On one occasion he stepped on one end of a loose plank and was hit in the face by the other end. At a circus, this scene might bring laughter and applause. But to Doctor Pinchus it was neither funny nor tragic.

There was nothing humorous about having to live in such a difficult place. He called his visits a *mitzvah,* a good deed, which called for no reciprocation. He didn't have to go there, but he wanted to. He suffered so many bumps, that one more didn't stop him. At no charge, he had an endless list of customers. He just put them into two categories: "Emergency" and "Can Wait." He was called "The Poor Man's Doctor," or "Pinchus the Medical Philanthropist." Some called him "The Cheap Doctor," although "reasonable" was the word they really meant.

Through the years, Dr. Pinchus built up such a name for himself rendering his services free, that even some of those who could afford to pay him didn't.

He never pressed for money. "Who knows" he used to say shrugging his shoulders and arms, "maybe something, God forbid, happened. Only God knows why this man can't afford to pay me." He felt obligated to the poor because, he would say, "They never had a chance."

When criticized by his non-paying patients for arriving late, he apologized. "Excuse me, I didn't mean to neglect you. I just came from a man who was in worse shape. If you could only see him you'd put on your prayer shawl and thank God for the shape you are in. Now, tell me what's bothering you?"

The poverty-stricken liked him not only because he saved their lives, but also for the way in which he did it. He had a way of reaching them on their own level. He was one of them; sort of a medical Don Quixote with more action than talk.

Everybody loved this man. Hundreds depended on him to keep them alive. Hundreds gave him their blessings. To scores of retarded, he was their only hope. The Nazis plucked him away from the needy and fenced him into a ghetto. There, they murdered him.

Those who still existed, looked like living corpses. The look of them alone was enough to drive one mad. They stood in the wind, huddled together to protect themselves against its force.

The helpless watched in horror as their friends fell like flies. They said nothing. They were too tired to give this meaningless life much thought. Nor was it any use to talk. What could they say to those who felt the same as they? It would be like talking to yourself, so why waste precious breath? Everyone's thoughts were the same: "Who's going to be next?" They didn't look for new friends. They were hoping that at least some of the old ones would be saved; someone to care about.

Their heartless masters had grown adjusted to their death assignments. They were taught and brainwashed into this sort of "solving" the problem of the Jews. The problem was created by the Nazi Doctrine and its "solution" became one of the duties of every "patriotic" German. The SS assigned pairs from among the human leftovers to pick up the starved.

"*Schnell, schnell,* faster," screamed the German officer. "They are beginning to stink."

Like a sack of garbage they were ordered to be picked up and dumped on stretchers. Some, still breathing, with eyes half closed, gazed almost motionlessly at their comrades carrying them alive into the pit. They were watching their own funerals, incapable of saying a word.

One woman tried to say something; she was trying to leave a message. But her head collapsed as she tried to turn it. Flies followed about her face, particularly her mouth, nostrils and the corner of the eyes. It was these insects who were the first to find out and tell the rest that she was dead.

A woman carrying a stretcher fell to her knees. Her

90

partner could not prevent the body from rolling off the stretcher and away from them.

Knowing the consequences, she rushed to raise her friend on her feet before the *polizai* and the Germans saw her. She tried twice to pick her up, but she kept falling. Her cry of despair was heard by an officer. With his cigar in one hand, and the other in his pocket, he casually walked over.

Lying on the ground, she saw his boots coming towards her. She took a deep breath and struggled to her knees. He pulled out his pistol from its holster and calmly said:

"Are you waiting till the bolsheviks come here and take you into heaven? I'm going to help you get there if you don't go back to work on the double."

Without waiting even a second he leveled the pistol at her head and fired. He motioned to another woman to take her place.

"Hey you, both of you, get these two rots on the stretcher, and from now on put two on each time. If I see only one body on the stretcher the two of you will make three."

The sight at the pit was unbelievable. It bespoke total disrespect for human life. Emaciated bodies were dumped like trash. A man was dropped on his head, a woman on her chest, a child on its face. All were piled one on top of another.

It was stunning evidence of the Nazi machinery at work; this was what their propaganda called a "Better Europe!"

Aaron recalled the days when he was a kid. How he used to watch the dog catchers chasing dogs, holding long sticks with a looped cord. They cornered the four-legged animals, set the loop and tightened it. The dog was caught by his stomach, legs, neck—all depending on his move. Once, Aaron saw one picked up by the throat. The dog catcher immediately took the choking dog and put him inside a wagon.

For some reason he always resented dog catchers although his mother told him that they are just doing their job for the city—trying to prevent little boys and girls from being bitten. "I never dreamed of dogs becoming man catchers," he thought to himself bitterly watching his two-legged Nazi master beasts.

Yet, it had happened.

10

THE CAMP WAS SURROUNDED by such a high concrete wall that no one could look in. It was braced by tall electrically charged barbed fences. Watch towers were all around. The whole place was lit up by a chain of strong lamps, and search-lights were installed on all towers.

Inside were blocks for prisoners, a kitchen, an administrative office and a hospital.

The prisoners looked like walking skeletons. They were often made to stand outside with their feet in cold water and mud. The SS, well fed and dressed comfortably, didn't blink an eye at their shivering bodies.

The overcrowding in the wet barracks added to the inevitable sickness. Dirt and stale air invited lice, spotted fever, typhus, and TB.

The hospital was always full, and when it became overcrowded many prisoners were put to death. There, Aaron was attached to the body-hauling command. Corpses were stocked up outside the hospital five feet high. They were naked. He felt like vomiting, but there was no food in his stomach. His detail of prisoners received for its offensive work an extra ration.

One prisoner ran a fever and couldn't jump to his feet when called by the SS commander. He was put into a tall wooden box with room for standing only. He went without food and water for a week. Before he died, he screamed his heart out and went insane.

Ten and eleven-year-old boys showed their muscles and flexed them before their executioners—"Look, Herr, I'm strong. I can work, please don't send me away. . . ." The answer was short. "Up into the truck!" A push and a kick hurried their fast departure.

Then there was the gassing.

Women with small children and other "unproductive" people were brought by trains. A large detachment of SS would be waiting to meet them. The victims were overwhelmed by exhaustion and misery and fear. Some of them had gone mad on the journey from fear, scratching their faces and pulling their hair.

"You are going to take a bath," they were told. "Then you'll get hot soup and bread. Leave your shoes and clothing together and in order so you can find them easily on your way out."

The condemned never got to use their clothes again. They never got the soup or bread either.

They were ordered inside a dark room fitted with showers. The doors were shut tight and the gas turned on. Wild screaming and pounding on the door could be heard.

Aaron watched as some were shot, some beaten, some trampled.

But something in him, something that would not forget the sweetness of life, kept him going, and he looked for a way to escape.

One day, inmates were told that the next morning at dawn they would be taken close to an airport. Their intuition told them that they would be shot. Hundreds hid in closets, basements, under mattresses, wherever possible.

At dawn, Nazis with their local Ukrainian helpers were already running, barking from barrack to barrack, picking up all the people for supposedly urgent work at the airport.

Aaron was among them. Each inmate was given a shovel. About fifty Ukrainian guards armed with rifles followed the SS camp leader. The camp inmates glared at each other trying to find consolation. Everybody was pale; some turned grey. Why would fifty men with fifty rifles follow only two hundred harmless people to work? The camp leader and his half-drunk cohorts hollered with excitement: *Eins, zwei, drei."* The *polizai*, well-dined and wined, used the butts of the rifles on the condemned. Those who fell from exhaustion received a bullet or two.

The inmates doubted if any one of them would make it to the contrived work area. Near a valley they were ordered to stop. They were ordered to dig a mass grave for the dead. Sand was mixed with roots, rags and papers. The shovels rang as they hit stones and pieces of brick.

A chill ran through Aaron's body.

After the digging was finished, they were ordered to bury the dead. "Go and get your friends!" the executioners screamed. They knew what was coming next. They looked and felt like living corpses. They could hardly move. Yet they carried some of the corpses for over half a mile.

Aaron picked up the body of a woman. He recognized her. He had just talked to her less than an hour ago. She had asked him if he had heard anything of her son, his best friend. He got the strange feeling of carrying his own mother. He looked upwards, in a gesture of prayer. The clouds moved about slowly shadowing the blue of the sky, as if they were trying to keep someone up there from seeing what was going on in the horrible world on earth. Never before had he looked for help so desperately.

He wondered if God could see or hear him. This was the crucial test of His presence. This was the time for proof. If He *is* Almighty, this was the moment to show His might for the sake of justice and use His power to save all these innocent souls. Aaron's mother suddenly entered his thoughts and he murmured to himself:

> *Let's be silent, even more silent*
> *Not one word said.*
> *Let's close our eyes*
> *And pray instead.*
>
> *No fences, no wires,*
> *Nor the SS guards;*

None can stop
Our crying hearts.

Just as you do to the trees,
Don't avoid us windy breeze.
All the prayers we say—
Please take them far away.

You are so refreshing, so fine.
Oh, you wind, wind of mine—
You'll warm my sick mother's heart
If you just send her my regard!

Among millions of eyes
You can tell hers—
They are always in tears.
No wind can dry them!
Lonesome like a stem
She thinks and thinks;
Whatever happened to me.

Hurry wind, make it snappy—
You can make her happy,
Send my message to her and then—
Her eyes will see her child again.

He went all cold inside. The dozen shovelfuls were the
hardest work of his life. This was too much for him; he
couldn't bring himself to look at it. He stood motionless.
The immovable faces of the guards drove him out of his
mind.

"Hurry up, hurry up!" the guards shouted.

Some were kicked, beaten by the Ukrainian *polizai* with
brutal viciousness and in a strange sadistic frenzy. They
hit everyone they could lay their hands on. He knew that
as soon as this job was completed, the rest of them would
meet the same fate. He was right. It didn't take more than
a few minutes; at a motion from the SS leader, a hail of
bullets poured over the condemned.

Screams of men, cries of women were mixed with the
rattle of the dying and the moans of the wounded. Aaron
brought his hands together and shrunk his shoulders in
shock, with his eyes closed and lips pressed tightly together,

96

waiting for a miracle. People huddled, clinging to one another helplessly. None of them expected to survive.

Aaron was fortunate. The first bullets missed him. He dove under a pile of dead and mortally wounded, and lay riveted to the spot. With one eye he saw a guard come closer to the pit shooting at anyone who seemed alive. His head sank a couple of more inches. They continued shooting at everything that moved or didn't. Then he heard the ringing of shovels and the sound of sand dropping over the bodies. The sand came closer to him and finally some of it filled his ear.

After several minutes the shooting stopped. Aaron turned very slowly and moved part of his head out from under the bodies. He saw one of the murderers snapping a photograph. They were evidently satisfied and had withdrawn.

By then Aaron was half crazed but his urge for life didn't weaken. "How much more can I stand?" he thought. "For the sake of life one can go through fire and water, but how can I go on?" One doesn't give up life as long as there is one breath left in him, and so Aaron sipped the heavenly air through an opening between the bodies. "All I have to do," he thought," is to keep myself from screaming, crying, moaning or breathing hard, and then? Who knows? I'll worry what to do then."

He was caked with dirt. His throat was dry and covered with blood. He saw the Ukrainian *polizai* march away singing loud songs with drunken voices and raising clouds of dust. At his side he saw a worm. He wondered what the worm thought. "Who is going to eat whom first?"

"Oh God," he cried out to himself, "how could you have split a sea, yet failed to stop a few murderers from pulling their triggers? Look, how did You allow it to happen to such good people? Some of them were so pious; they served You faithfully all their lives? *Oy*, how could You?" He could hear no answer.

"Maybe God helps those who help themselves?"

He couldn't wait until it got dark. The odor from the dead was unbearable. He looked around. No one alive was in sight. He picked his way out of the death pit and climbed over bodies which were almost completely silent.

Reluctantly, Aaron stepped over them, trying to make his way out of the pit. As he took one more cautious look toward the outside he heard heavy breathing coming from the mass grave. A dizziness entered his head and his body became numb. He looked down. It was Berle, the tailor, a lifelong friend of the family. He bent over and whispered to him. "Berle, hey Berle." But Berle couldn't hear. Berle was dead.

For another minute Aaron sat startled and scared, not knowing what to do. Then he remembered. He was alive! Yes, alive. The breathing was his own. Weak from hunger and deadly scared, but alive. What does a human being do at a time like this?

"Run and hide, his mind dictated. You must survive for a very important reason. If they get you, no one in the whole world will be able to tell what they did. I wonder if the world will believe me? Yes, it will. It will have to!"

Without looking back, he dashed into the woods in blind terror. The dry grass and fallen branches crunched under foot. It was getting dark. He wanted to turn around, but he couldn't bring himself to look at the massacre again. In the woods he stretched out his feet and arms, and straightened out his neck. For a minute or so he was gulping for air. Dazed but alive, his mind began to clear. He needed to live! "Let's see now? Where do I go from here?"

To his left, a mile or two away, was a village; to the right a few barns; behind him the camp.

He tried to see farther ahead of him. There was nothing in sight except for something that looked like a small river. Yes, a river; that's it. "First, I must cleanse myself of the blood."

He walked cautiously. Being spotted by someone could be disastrous.

"Why?" he asked himself. "Why should I be fearful? I haven't done anything wrong."

But there was no time for logic. A soft wind carried the sounds of laughing hyenas. It didn't sound like laughter to him. Their howling reminded him more of children crying out of desperation. The beasts let themselves be heard from several directions while looking and rummaging for prey. "A child's cry I haven't heard in years. Perhaps they were already stifled." This thought and a lullabye ran through his mind:

> Close your eyes, the big, the deep,
> And go, baby, to sleep.
> The enemy wants to hurt you by all means,
> And you don't know for what kind of sins.

> All they have for you in store
> Is the tragedy of war;
> They can't win,
> They just sin and sin.

> Your daddy was sent away,
> Your mommie was lucky to stay
> So sleep angel, just for you
> Mommie can live; this is true.

> The time will come, oh God,
> When you'll be big and strong;
> You'll take revenge
> For your people's sweat and blood.

He rushed from tree to tree towards the river. Fallen pine cones, the kind his mother placed inside the samovar and then heated it, lay all around.

His last stop was a heavy bush. He crouched inside and peeked out. The bank of the river was deserted; it was hugged by waves powered by a light wind. As he tried to get up he felt as if he had a load of concrete on his back. He was only about twenty, but he felt old.

The slight wind almost swept him off his feet. He saw the leaves shiver along with him. Even they were around their family tree. He was shaky and so were his chances for survival.

Aaron could hear his heart beat. It was strong for such a weak body. It sounded like thunder as he went towards the water. He knelt and lowered his exhausted face into the cool water several times. He scooped it into his dried out hands as if it were liquid gold. It refreshed him. He drank and drank. For a while, he felt as if he could drink forever. But the murmur of the water unsteadied him. And every noise of nature rubbed at the edges of his frazzled nerves.

His flimsy camp jacket was splashed with blood. He stripped it off, washed it and put it on again wet. This was all he had. He needed it to protect himself. Like a wet handkerchief, it stuck to his shivering body. His teeth were chattering. He felt the relief of cleanliness. Feeling like a new person for just a few moments, Aaron began to see more light. The river water had hit the spot. It tasted like quinine water with an indescribable flavor. It opened the walls of his shrunken stomach and cleared his mind at the same time.

His main thought was not to be seen by anyone. Shelter and food were next. He had difficulty in holding his head straight. Falling asleep in the wrong place or at the wrong time could mean falling into the hands of the SS and certain death.

There was only one way for Aaron to go and that was to the deserted barn a little distance away with no house nearby. An open area for about a few hundred feet was just ahead. He tried to run, but his tired legs wouldn't let him. Groggily, he swayed like a drunkard. As he neared the barn he heard the loud moo of a cow. It sounded like music compared to the barking of the human beasts he had just escaped from.

Inside, he found a conglomeration of more sounds from cows, goats and pigs. Each one of them seemed to be voicing his opinion at intervals. The animal odor was overpowering. Aaron remembered his father, once hearing him complain about a pig sty, saying: "Just smell out your share, son, and be quiet."

For a while he observed, in the dark, the peaceful silhouettes of the animals. There was not one human soul besides himself. He felt relieved. He had never realized before that a man could feel so safe among animals, and so unsafe among people. He lay down in a corner hoping none of these domestic animals would step on him.

He never dreamed he would find himself clinging to life in a barn. His eyes shut instantly and he slept soundly.

Aaron was awakened by the serenade of a rooster. He saw his animal friends again. For the first time he felt how refreshing the odor from animals could be, and how contaminating the presence of people. "What irony," he cried to himself.

There were several dozen animals there, but none paid any special attention to him, and the first thought that entered his mind was: "What can I share with them by way of food?"

His eyes lit up! A whole pile of corncobs was at one cow's feet. He crawled over near it and looked up at the cow. She looked back at him. "You aren't going to kick me, are you?" He thought to himself. "Of course not, you probably wouldn't care if a hungry man took one or two . . . your master will bring more. . . ." He eyed her with jealousy: "How I envy you! How I would like to change places with a contented cow like you!"

He took a corn in his mouth like a harmonica, and the chewing sounded like the sweetest music he had heard in a long time. Accompanied by the crowing of the cocks and the squeal of an awakening pig it all sounded like an opera to him. He couldn't have asked for a finer feast. He waited for the cow to get through drinking water from a pail. There was some left. Just enough for a drink and a wash for his weary face, overgrown by a heavy beard.

Aaron realized that this self-picked sanctuary was safe only for a short while. He knew he couldn't stay there for much longer although he wouldn't mind. The master should be coming there any time, maybe any minute. Someone must be tending these fine animals.

Aaron climbed a ladder and looked around. He had a bird's eye view. There was not a house in sight. Suddenly, he noticed something that made him rub his eyes. A limping man was walking out from behind a hill, and a little girl followed him. Aaron was dumbfounded. He didn't know what to do. He thought to himself, "I just can't give myself up. They may turn me in and it will be the end of me. Anyway, I need more time to think, to make some sound plans and decisions."

He quickly looked up and then climbed into the loft, littered with straw. Right above him an ugly spider sat with several flies in his cruel web. He reminded Aaron of the Nazis constantly trapping their human victims into a trap of deceit and then death. By instinct Aaron quickly shoved the spider down to the floor, wishing it were possible to do the same to the Nazis.

"No one can see me up here," he said to himself, "and as for the animals, such good Samaritans and loyal friends, they wouldn't squeal." He lay practically without breathing, hoping that he wouldn't cough or sneeze because of the strong hay odor, but he didn't.

The man and girl walked inside and greeted their animals in Polish. The girl tapped some of them on their rear ends, calling them by their names. The farmer sat down at the milking stool. The girl handed him the pail, and the milk started to squirt. When it was full, he picked up the pail and the two walked back home. When their silhouettes disappeared behind the hill, Aaron crawled down.

He stretched his arms as he browsed around, getting acquainted with the animals. A goat was chewing away, and looked at him as if he were a stranger from paradise. Two pigs were sunning in an odor-drenched mud hole, rubbing their bodies and touching faces. Even pigs could find love in a world of hate. He found sheets of old newspapers scattered around. Printed in Polish, it showed the Germans over and over again victorious throughout Europe.

He lost track of how many days he lived together with the friendly animals in the barn. He was not in a hurry to leave. It was the best home he had enjoyed in two years. With all the noise and mess, it still felt like heaven.

Aaron kept thinking of the whereabouts of his parents, his brother and his friends. Occasionally, he talked in a soft voice to them.

The fear of death, which builds up from hour to hour,

102

is hard to endure. A man has only one life. And the first one to suspect—man, woman, or child would report him. His mother's words rang in his ears. "Some learn to live as they were treated." They used to say his dog, Klinky, was treated so well he thought he was human. Aaron wished he could change places with him. But how could he compare himself with Klinky. The dog was surrounded with love and Aaron with hate. His dog's life was guarded at all times, and his own threatened every minute.

He wondered if Klinky missed him?

With all his masters tossed into concentration camps, where is he now? Is he rummaging over the garbage cans, settling for something he wouldn't touch at home, this spoiled *shlemiel?* Or, is he perhaps shivering from cold and howling at strangers' doors, crying for a warm place to rest in? With his irresistable eyes, there is even a chance that a Nazi officer may have him in his quarters. Imagine this little traitor shifting to the enemy. Could he ever blame him—his four-legged best friend—for betraying him? If the two-legged species did it, why couldn't a four-legged one do the same, he continued to muse.

Aaron thought he would rather see him being fed by a human beast than being killed. Would he ever see Klinky again? Such a silly thought to travel through one's mind at a time like this. But what else is there to pass the time? He kept pushing into the back of his head the horrible things that might have happened, but somehow they kept coming back. Uninvited and as unwelcome as they were, they kept bouncing back like a ball on a tin roof.

"Memories! How sweet they were!" This was all that was left. This was his only luxury. To him it was like a bottle of wine which intoxicated him and brought him into a new world; a world of fantasy in which he found himself as a new man.

Aaron once thought of Yoske, a Communist, who received five years at hard labor for throwing a Red flag up over an electric street wire on May first. For his father's funeral he was given half a day off. Aaron remembered his gray face and grieving eyes staring at the clumsy street stones.

Guarded by two armed, uniformed men, he put his hand on the casket as if trying to touch his father and relay a message. He looked crushed from swinging a sledge hammer over granite stones, and he was broken up by the death of his father. His heart was crying, but his sunken eyes remained tearless, focused upon his father's bier.

The distant relatives and friends bore the coffin, made out of rough boards crudely nailed together. Through a gap between the boards Yoske looked at the body of his father. There he lay, peacefully, with his eyelids closed and mouth tightly shut. The body was wrapped in his prayer shawl, his fringed *Talis*. A white cap covered his balding head, and white stockings were put upon his legs.

They passed by the Choir Shul, the noted synagogue on Zawalna street where his father came every Sabbath and holiday to listen to the children's velvet voices. There he enjoyed the cantor as he chanted the blessings so beautifully. At this picturesque synagogue the procession halted and a prayer was recited. A short eulogy was delivered. "A man who suffers in this world gets relief in heaven," said the rabbi.

Yoske wasn't one who believed in the heavenly angels, but he seemed to derive a sense of comfort out of this ceremony.

Before placing the body in its final resting place the departed soul was asked to forgive any wrong and to depart in peace from the world.

A grief-stricken mumble softly streamed out of Yoske's mouth: "Pa, hey Pa. Too bad you can't hear me. You probably wouldn't believe me anyway if I told you how I'm being treated and for what? Just for throwing a Red flag on a wire. No one got hurt. Perhaps I should have thought of it, but I didn't mean to cause you that heartache. Pa, honestly I didn't. . . . You may have not agreed with me on Communism, but I believed in it. I don't feel sorry for myself. I'm only sorry that I couldn't help you load up your pushcart. It was your bread and butter. This bothered me. But how does the saying go? 'The Pole gets wise after the damage.' But what can I do now? I can only remember it as long as I live and that, too, may not be so long. With Mom passing away last year, you were alone for a solid year—three hundred and sixty-five days.

"I was thinking of you at all times. For you, I was the only one left alive, and yet dead as the rest of the family. Such a shame you can't hear me. . . . Maybe it's better. . . . The things that happen to me daily shouldn't happen to a dog. It's better you never knew it, or did you have a hunch? You must have known that they don't serve chicken soup and cake over there.

"Did any of the notes I tried to slip through ever reach you? I wish you could answer me on that.

"Well, Pa, it's over now."

The body was lowered and people took turns casting earth into the grave until it was filled. Mourning for his father was supposed to last one year. The law called for no work for the first seven days after a death in the family, but to Yoske, a man considered by the prison authorities to be a Red atheist, this privilege would probably not be granted.

He remembered the week of daily prayers following the death of his father. True, he didn't believe in them, but do they hurt? After all, they are for his father who expected him to say *Kadish*, the prayer for the soul. . . . Papa didn't call him "my *Kadish* sayer" for nothing.

As for wearing leather footwear during the *Shivah*, the seven days of mourning, that, Papa would probably forgive him under the circumstances. But, *Kadish*. . . .

"I wish I had learned the prayer by heart. What if I ask the prison guard to get me a Hebrew prayerbook? Instead, the anti-Semite will add a jolt to my broken body and an insult to my open wound."

And what about *Yorcajt*, the anniversary of death he and Papa so faithfully observed after Mama. How could he forget that *Yorcajt*? He is going to go back where he'll remember it every day of his life.

On days when life goes out like a candle burning on both sides, where else can a human being lean for good memories

105

if not on his parents? Who else will understand his bitter heart? Who else will be so gracious as to forgive him?

Aaron remembered the moment of Yoske's parting, with friends kissing him on both cheeks. This warmth melted his icy heart. Yoske was overwhelmed and broke into tears. His heart was broken and he wept bitter tears.

A friend pressed him in his arms, tears flowing fast. He whispered in his ear. "Keep your head up, Yoske. Remember the saying: If you have lost your money you haven't lost anything; but if you have lost your spirit you have lost everything."

Aaron looked up, turned his eyes toward the blue sky and said:

> *Oh, God Almighty:*
> *Lend me two wings*
> *To fly away*
> *From the evil*
> *You oppose.*
>
> *Turn me into a wind*
> *That I may blow away*
> *From the human disgrace*
> *That you feel and face*
> *(Remember I'm one*
> *Of the people you chose).*
>
> *Make me a hog*
> *So I could eat*
> *All I can,*
> *Make me a dog*
> *To be loved by man.*
>
> *Make me a bird*
> *So I can sing*
> *And be happy as a lark.*
> *Make me a tree*
> *That's blooming,*
> *And feel safe under its bark.*
>
> *God Almighty:*
> *Please make me anything*
> *But not a human being.*

One night Aaron was awakened by voices.

At first he thought it was a nightmare, but he heard whispering, then footsteps. The barn door squeaked, and he saw the dark shadows of several men walking inside. His heart sank. He froze. He felt numb, paralyzed, and he almost stopped breathing. With his head clinging to the loft board, he glanced down and from the side of his eye, saw a flash of light.

A soft voice in Polish asked: "Let's see if someone is sleeping in here."

"Are they looking for me? Maybe they heard me snoring."

The spot of the flashlight probed every corner of the barn. Like a spirit he shrank, trying to make himself invisible.

He heard someone being called "Commander." Then another said: "Comrade." One was holding an automatic.

"They kind of look like partisans," he thought. "Maybe they can help me. Maybe I can follow them in the woods."

"Hi, boys," he mumbled.

"Where are you? Stay where you are!" they shouted, scared and surprised.

"I'm here, upstairs."

A flashlight, after wandering in search, spotted Aaron's face, and a gun was focused against it. Aaron climbed down, his face blinded by the glare of the bright light.

Looking at the striped, shabby concentration camp outfit one man said: "What are you doing here?"

Too old to cry and too shaken to keep calm, Aaron choked up. It was just too much for him. Warm tears of happiness rolled down his cheeks.

"Don't worry son," said the mustached leader, we are all in the same boat now. We'll outlive the Nazis yet; and if not, an honorable death is better than dying on your knees. Our parents didn't die for nothing—they brought us up properly. They gave us strength to go on. Those of us who weren't destroyed got stronger, and now we are willing to help our brothers and sisters. It will take time. We are in this deadly game even if it means a lifetime."

Aaron was filled with pride as he listened to these words.

The partisans picked up corn and milked a few cows. "That's Wiggle, my favorite cow," Aaron said.

"How do you know her name?" one of the armed men asked curiously.

"I gave her the name because whenever she looked at me she wiggled her tail."

It was time to go. "Good-bye Wiggle. Sorry to leave you."

"Where are we going?" Aaron asked.

"When we get there you'll find out. You are now a soldier of a secret army located in a secret place. A cruel war is going on with tremendous odds against us. We are surrounded by the worst kind of enemy the twentieth century has ever known. He has defeated and captured over a dozen countries, and our group is only a David trying to fight Goliath.

"Who knows how long we are going to be forced to fight our own little battle with the enemy."

One of the partisans handed Aaron a piece of bread. He looked at it in the dark. It looked like gold. Even more! It was priceless.

It tasted just like honey cake.

He began to calm down. He looked up at them. They looked as if they were made of granite—strong and straight. These men faced death every hour, yet were unafraid. They faced an enemy of unmatched superiority in manpower and weapons. These were brave men, men who were not afraid to die; true heroes.

"Thanks for taking me with you," Aaron said with a trembling voice; his knees wobbly. They could see that Aaron was in a state of shock, yet they were not moved by it. They were tough, hardened by their daily experiences. He felt honored being among these heroic men.

Suddenly, he felt under his arms two hands helping him up the hill. His throat was dry. He was handed a canteen with water. A few gulps forced the precious bread down his throat. He tried to raise his head and straighten his

108

shoulders, but he couldn't. The burden of the last difficult days was too heavy to get rid of so soon. The Commander noticed his effort and said: "All right, son. Everything will be all right."

11

THE NEXT DAY Aaron listened to his first lesson from the Partisans.

"Today we are going to learn subversion," the commander said.

"An assignment must be carried in the head. You don't write anything down. When you are on a mission, you don't carry arms, except when your assignment is to kill somebody.

"You must look and act cool; just as if you have no intention of doing anything unusual. You must not let your fears throw you into panic. You are touching bottom, and when you are that low there is only one way to go—up. You realize that you are as small as a fly and that your life is nothing. Not when you measure it by thousands of lives depending on you and me.

"You don't feel ashamed of how dirty or bloody your hands will turn, as long as the blood is that of the enemy."

"You must rid yourself of any guilt. This would interfere with your efficiency. Use positive thinking. You walk with your chin up, thinking to yourself that you are great, confident. Above all, you can't afford to look suspicious or make a mistake.

You don't think of yourself as a spoiler, a killer, but as a man with morals and goals. Not as a blabber but as a man of action—and action is stronger than words. Not as a coward hiding in a cave and living on roots, but as a man going out to fight for freedom; as an underground soldier fighting his way through to victory. You are not a mouse, but a man, one out of a million. Think only of what you can do to harm the enemy, and you won't have time to pity yourself.

"Just think of how many lives you can save by killing the enemy. Tell yourself: You are alive and you'll live forever. Wrap yourself in good luck. Hurrah!

"This job is not easy. In peacetime a spy can get away with murder. Then a man can get a break. His country, which is on speaking terms with his captors, will try to defend him, minimize his crime and maybe even make a deal to trade him for one of theirs.

"In war, there is no footsying around. When you get caught you have two choices. You get shot the same day, or they'll prolong your life for another few hours, or even an extra day, if you'll spill out everything you know.

"The first choice will be an easier and more honorable way for you. Before you are sent on a mission you must know that the odds are heavy against you. To the underground fighter there are two kinds of death. The death of a soldier and the death of a coward. You, an amateur, are going to have to outsmart and outmaneuver professionals.

"When you expect the worst, you can't be disappointed. So expect death, and every day you remain alive, consider it a privilege. You are not scared of anything. When sentenced to death and trying to break out of the death chamber, you'll have to grab at the faintest chance. Now you are living like a vegetable, only trying to be a man. You see death? Keep your eyes wide open and you will see life.

"There is something more you need, to succeed. You need to disassociate yourself from reality. Don't think of your problems. You need faith with a capital F. You need a blessing, and you take anything that comes along that will help your spirit."

Aaron knew that some of this good group would be

killed. But those who would survive will really be the chosen people.

Square-shouldered, freckled and stocky, Igor handed Aaron a gun and said:

"You are a partisan from now on. Hold on to the gun. It may save your life. Keep it clean at all times, cherish it as if it were your baby. That's the only friend you have if you want to hope for survival."

Aaron had never handled a real gun before. It looked so ugly in the hands of the enemy. But this was different. This time it was in his possession.

The rifle was his mascot, his pride, his security, his baby, everything positive. Here he was to learn to kill. He had never thought of killing anyone, but he had heard it said:

"This is it, young man. To kill the enemy is the name of the game. And you better listen and hear so you can do to the Germans what they want to do to you. You must kill in order to survive."

The first few days Aaron didn't think he was strong enough to be a partisan. But he thought of the others in the death pit, and he soon learned.

Those who died at sixteen never saw seventeen. He had already seen twenty and he might see twenty-one. It already felt like a bonus.

He often felt he was talking to himself. He heard his buddies talk in their sleep, and figured he probably did too.

Life as a partisan was not an easy adjustment for a boy brought up in a warm home environment. The early stage of the partisan life was the most difficult for Aaron. The pressure of his emotions was too great. He had to unload them on paper. It came in the form of poetry.

IF I EVER SURVIVE

The day seems like a year;
A year—like a lifetime.
How can I be happy
Living in cold and in fear?

112

I want to live to see a child;
Pick it up in the air
Just to see it smile;
To hear its voice
How I would rejoice!

Man, oh, man,
I'd say hello
To every gloomy fellow,
Tap him on the shoulder
And say,
Hey! Isn't it good to be alive!
If I ever survive . . .

On cold nights especially, when he heard shooting nearby, he couldn't fall asleep. Who did the Germans hit with their bullets? Certainly not their comrades. He knew that. Their targets were more likely his people, his flesh and blood. He thought about his grandmother. Where was she? And David?

In the ghettos, bread rations were very skimpy and no other food was given. Whoever had an opportunity swapped his last belongings for a bit of extra food to stay alive. For a little piece of smuggled-in meat or butter, people gave away their best clothing and most valuable belongings. When caught by the guards they paid for it with their lives.

How does grandmother manage with food?—he wondered.

Writing poetry provided a way of overcoming the tension.

An old woman knocks on the door;
"Open please, you good people—
A whole day I haven't eaten,
I got forgotten by the Lord."

Good people, please listen to me—
I'll wash your shirts,
My clothes were taken from me
By the polizai.

Dear people, don't mind my nagging—
I'm not the only one that's begging—
You have a roof over your head—
I don't have a piece of bread.

There Aaron met a partisan friend, Sholem. On a gloomy evening Aaron listened to his new friend tell of his escape.

". . . I decided to run away from certain death. First it seemed to me it was just a little fantasy passing through my mind. What was needed was courage, ability, character, common sense!

"I wasn't sure I had it all, but I decided to take a crack at it anyway. How does the saying go? 'When a man is drowning he grabs the straw.'

"It happened during work on a grey rainy day. I slipped out and dashed into a thick forest. I ran for almost a whole day. It seemed endless.

"I tried to push my insecurity far back in my mind, but it kept popping up. Not for one minute could I forget myself. I pretended to be someone else, but it didn't work.

"I tried to recapture the love I had felt at home, to recall the times when I was considered a human being and treated like one. I tried to think of an idea. My lips shaped into a faint smile when I recalled my father saying: 'A good idea is a million dollars, and a million dollars is a good idea.'

" 'Only God knows,' my grandfather used to say, 'how long a man is going to live.' He was seventy-four and prayed at least three times a day. I'm praying for a hundred years and then if I feel good I'll ask Him for a few more.

"I listened to the babbling of the brook which spoke of love as it tumbled past into the rushing river. From a distance I kept hearing the call which inched into my heart. I was afraid of fatigue. It threatened to sap my strength, and I was fearful of becoming useless. I had to force myself to keep from dozing off. My nostrils twitched at the smell of seaweed. The sea breeze sighed as it passed through the pines.

"How I envied the local farmers their freedom to breathe in at all times; how I wanted to be in their place at least for a little while. How jealous I was of their coming home to a covered table, of being with their whole family; sitting down when they wished, saying what they pleased, singing as loud as they wished.

"I heard voices from inside the forest and ducked among

114

the bushes. It was a farm woman talking to a little girl. They were looking for mushrooms. My striped inmate's uniform . . . a child can't keep a secret. . . . But they passed by without seeing me. . . .

"At one end it looked as if more light was coming through. Perhaps it was the end of the forest. Like a four-legged animal, I climbed up a tree and began to observe—a few cows chewing peacefully on the grass, two little boys riding a horse, a hen chasing a few chicks, and a couple of goats playing with their horns. A woman carrying two pails of water was heading in my direction, but couldn't see me. On the other side I saw a lone wagon with something in it that looked like a grey sack. I climbed down from the tall tree without a scratch. I didn't know what to do next. I became weak from the lack of proper food and water. My stomach ached and my throat was dry. I weighed the possibilities in my mind. It was like an important conference with a smart man.

"I decided to make a bold move. Step by step I sneaked toward the wagon. Inside I found a pair of pants. They were the pants of a free man; plain color, no stripes. They had a few rips and patches, but still . . . not of an inmate.

"The woman working on her knees and facing the other way was unaware of me. I took the old clothing back into the bushes and changed. The pants were sizes too large and I had to hold them up with both hands. Time began to work against me. I was weak from the lack of food. I had to get going, but where?

"Pale and unshaven, but with my head up, I came up to her. 'Good day. My name is Boleslav Korczak. I am from the secret police. We were informed that partisans were around here recently.'

"She got up on her feet and gave me a good looking over from top to bottom. A slight blush of shocked surprise covered her face. I could read the distrust in her eyes. I didn't expect her to believe me. But in order to find my destination, I had no other choice. My approach was flimsy, but it was just about my only way of finding out where the partisans were without putting her life in jeopardy. To take me for a policeman or a detective she would have to be blind and deaf. Even a village idiot wouldn't trust a barefooted police official, nor could anyone mistake my Jewish accent."

Slightly shocked from this surprise visit, the woman tried to contain herself and to keep calm. She looked around and seemed to feel better when there was no one around to see and bear witness. She revealed her awareness of the situation as she went on with her work and talked casually, as though he were not there.

"They were here just a few days ago, on Friday I think."

"Which way did they go?"

"Down there across the river, up the hills, between the fallen tree and the creek."

"Thank you, mama," I said raising my hand. Our eyes met. There was a smile in my eyes and a tear in hers. The word mama had touched her deeply. Who knows if she, too, may not have had a son far from home, searching for life.

I walked past fields and down to the river. I swam over with my clothes on. There was no time for drying out. I looked back. Here and there farmers could be seen going about their own business. A windmill lazily kept moving in circles, a dog chasing a cat. Standing in ankle-deep water, a little boy was trying to fish with a crooked branch. On the other side of the river a German soldier amused himself with a local girl.

I tried not to pay attention. Like a bird toward his nest, I headed toward my landmark. There was the fallen tree in the creek. I drank and drank. Then I washed my face and drank again. It was a relief and a luxury of a special sort.

With new strength I straightened up my back. Up the hill I trudged with nothing in sight.

I decided to climb a tree and watch. I sat up there and looked for a camp, or at least something that would lead me towards the partisans. There was nothing but trees and more trees. I went down and looked for berries. There were none. I thought of going back to this reliable woman and ask for food. She at least knew who I was. On the other hand, I thought, may be I shouldn't. Why put her in jeopardy? She may not even be there, for that matter.

No, I just couldn't go back. I couldn't afford to be seen twice by anyone. I might trap myself that way. Why invite more trouble? The chill from the wet clothing began to get the better of me. My hunger grew and my body began to weaken. The moon gradually sank, and soon it hid behind the horizon.

It was a chilly, dark night. The quiet of the forest was occasionally interrupted by the howl of wolves. I was scared and instantly climbed a tree. After awhile I became uncomfortable sitting there. I knew for sure that I couldn't possibly sleep up there without falling off. This added to my stress. I began to sob and pull my hair. At the same time, I knew this would get me nowhere. I climbed down and tried to fall asleep. I couldn't find a comfortable spot. My thoughts hounded me.

Time was working against me. I knew I wouldn't be any further tomorrow. How did I know the woman in the field had kept our meeting to herself? Maybe her husband or one of the children would decide to talk. They were probably told how I looked and where I went. Their *polizai* may start an early morning search for me. Tomorrow may be too late.

I looked around and climbed the tallest tree, breaking some of my fingernails. I didn't know how to attract the partisans' attention. I whistled as loud as I could, but all I heard was my own echo.

I was going to holler, *pobeda*, a Russian word for victory, but I was afraid it might attract the wrong people instead. I had never been so confused and undecided in my whole life. I just had to make a move. I picked the word, *prikhozhu*, I'm coming. Again no other echo but my own.

As I had all but given up, I saw a little fire flicker. I climbed down and began to go in that direction. It could have been the police or a local forest crew. Helplessly undecided, I didn't know what to do or where to turn for help. This could be the fire of my last hope or the fire that would roast me alive.

117

As I followed in this direction I lost sight of the little fire. Suddenly I heard a voice; Hold it! A tall man pointed a rifle at me. Hands up!

The command came in Polish. I raised both my hands up with relief. I knew it was not the police as the man was dressed in an old, long Russian overcoat.

"Who are you? Where did you come from? Who told you we were around here?"

"At first I was speechless; then I began to mumble.

"He soon found out that I was all right, the kind they were looking for to fill in their shrinking manpower. 'Follow me, son, I'll take you to our fighting unit.'

How did you find me? I asked.

"I followed you for the last couple of hours. From atop a tree I spotted you through my field glasses swimming across the river, the man said.

"Making it across the deep waters with your clothing on gave me the first hint that you may be one of our future boys. But in our position we can't afford to take chances. We must really be sure.

"My second clue was when you emerged barefoot and looked around suspiciously as if you were scared of the authorities. I heard you whistle, and I wasn't sure what you were up to. I saw you climbing up and down the tree. You could have been a double crosser, but when you didn't return before dark and I heard you weeping, I went back and told them to light a tiny fire so you would know in what direction to go. I myself wasn't sure exactly how to find you, but expected you to come this way. So I hid behind a tree and waited until you came real close.

"The group of underground warriors lay on coats, straw and soft branches. It was pitch dark. I couldn't see their faces, only their silhouettes. They all looked great and beautiful."

Sholem developed his own system of overcoming the dragging hours. He talked without a stop. He was called the self-winding, talking machine.

Most of his talk was nonsense, and at first some considered him a clown or a fool. But as the partisans got to

118

know him better they realized that there is nothing wrong with a man talking excessively as long as he does not step on anyone's toes. His audience began to increase and all seemed to enjoy his company. What can be wrong with any man who makes people happy or makes them forget? In good times anyone can be happy, but it takes a special man to be gay and laugh when death is just around the corner. "What is there to look for in life," Sholem used to philosophize, "except for happiness? It makes no difference how you obtain it as long as you get it." He used to have a group of definitions of happiness: Happiness is to see an SS man with his hands up and pants down. Happiness is to see a Nazi who discovers his inferiority. Happiness is to see a captured turncoat turning in his underwear.

With the partisans, a man lived like an animal, struggling from hour to hour, day to day. There was just a dim present and no future.

Yet, there was a future to think about. At least the thought of it brought a spark of joy to Aaron's heart. He would wrap himself into a web of fantasy and daydream. It didn't cost him anything and any daydream is better than a nightmare. Who wanted to think of nightmares? Life in the woods, sneaking away from the Germans, was a nightmare in itself.

Daydreaming was about all there was left to soothe the worn nerves. It was the only tonic for broken hearts.

A man born free just isn't used to that kind of life. He yearns to be free, and when he can't be, he learns to become a slave—only with difficulty.

A man prefers to be with his kin, but when forced away, he looks for the nearest thing to it. There is no substitute for kin, but a man is not an island. He may sometimes play the role of being all alone; but not for long. He needs someone to be with, to look at, someone to talk to him and hear him answer.

He is thus created, a creature to be with and share with others. He can be his own island for a while; talk to himself and live on grass roots, but the toll soon catches up with him.

The townspeople were already indoctrinated by the Nazis to hate the partisans and to turn them over to the executioners. They were warned on every occasion that the price for turning in a Jew was ten marks; death for not reporting one.

Aaron looked at the people around him, people like himself, trying to survive. He felt great, and important. He could talk to his superior sitting down and take orders without being abused. He began to feel like a new person.

He saw a new world of danger, but one he could take pride in. Without a calendar or watch he didn't even know the day or the time. But who cared? A day seemed like a year and a year, a lifetime. He saw a blond boy, not more than sixteen, cleaning a rifle. A man, nude from the waist up, rubbed his selfmade razor against the inside of his belt trying to sharpen it for a shave. Another was reading a book, and two others were chatting. A broad-shouldered young man in his early twenties was crooning a Polish love song. A girl with a red cross on her arm was busy preparing breakfast. Sholem was armed with eating utensils consisting of a bent tin cup, a spoon and a hammered out tin fork of non-symmetrical proportions.

It was a "come and get it" breakfast consisting of a good size piece of slightly stale dark bread with a smearing of jam made from berries picked in the surrounding area.

Soon after came his initiation. It was short and informal. The oath was: "I swear to humanity that I will defend my land from the German invaders. Regardless of all danger, I swear to obey every order of my superior commander. I swear that I'll never give my comrades away. I'm ready to give my blood and my life if necessary. I'll fight till my last breath."

After repeating word after word, a soft traditional applause followed from the comrades.

"I pronounce you a partisan of the Sokolovka Unit," said the commander.

Getting to know more about the partisans, Aaron realized that it takes a brave man to be a partisan. They live in a world in which life is cheap. It is hard for them to be taken care of medically; and they are even harder to re-place. Out of a group of seventeen there were several Russian officers including his commander, who had been trapped by Germans at the beginning of the war and decided to form a partisan group instead of surrendering to the Germans. Their Red Army uniforms were so worn out and faded from the sun that they looked like prisoners. There was Doctor Katia, a short, chubby hook-nosed Russian woman. In incredibly difficult conditions, without proper instruments or medical supplies or even bandages, she managed to save many lives of the partisans.

A few Poles, one Lithuanian, formerly minor officials in the Red dominated government also joined. The official partisan language was Russian, since all knew how to speak it.

They usually kept quiet, although any one of them would have plenty to tell if asked. Everyone could have written a book about his adventures.

The losses suffered by the partisans were extremely heavy, but no matter how many died they still carried on.

The German blitz didn't give them much of a chance. Right from the beginning they were encircled and wiped out. Many died of cold, hunger and illness in their forest camps. Many more died of wounds, some light, because they had no doctor and hardly any medication.

The atrocities committed against the captured partisans and suspected partisan sympathizers rank among the worst kind committed by the Germans.

One day Red intelligence helicopters reached the partisans by radio, then spotted out the location.

The good news gave the partisans wings. The day and time was not given to them for security reasons.

"Just hang around," they were told, "we will be there to see you."

One night they were awakened by a soft motor noise. They all jumped up, grabbed weapons and ran the short distance of perhaps fifty feet. They saw the air-bird land just like a chicken between low pine trees. It raised a storm of leaves and grass all over the place.

121

The Reds took no chances either.

With automatic weapons in their hands, they called for the commander. After a short conversation, and identification of papers, the rest of the partisans were asked to come closer.

With a customary Russian-style speech, he started: "Friends, brothers and sisters. We, a unit of the Red Armed Forces, come to tell you that you are not alone. We know about you and look up to you as our comrades-in-arms.

"We have brought you food, the same rations military forces receive. We have brought you up-to-date arms so you can help us successfully to defeat the bestial enemy. We have warm clothing for you. We are going to leave two of our friends here with you. Comrade Captain Bari is a radio specialist. He'll keep in touch with us. He'll help guide your security, and will provide communication with us. Also to stay is Comrade Lieutenant Ivanov. He is a doctor and he'll be of great help to you. So much for now. For security reasons we cannot stay here longer. Goodnight and good luck. Keep up your good work. We'll see you again and again until we all celebrate the final victory over the destruction of Nazism."

One evening they drank hot tea with *prekuska*, a hard, clumsy lump of sugar which gradually melts down with each swallow. Sholem glanced at Bari's chest and asked him what all the five medals were for.

"Those are for fighting off a village full of sex-hungry girls," he kibitzed, humbly. "But all kidding aside, after I came here I became convinced that for every medal an army man gets, a partisan should be getting three."

Aaron was impressed with his modesty and he said, "I can't see myself getting any medals whatsoever."

"What do you mean?" Bari asked.

"I haven't seen anyone getting a medal for sleeping, eating and loafing."

"But wait a minute, you already deserve one for making it over here; and by the time the war will be over you'll deserve many more. And what is a medal? Just a piece of tin," said Bari.

"Fighting against Nazism for humanity is the highest award." Vaitras, a Lithuanian partisan, wanted to know why more Jews did not join the fight.

Aaron told him, that the Jews in the camps, unlike others, are under constant surveillance.

"This I know," Vaitras said. "But being the most oppressed by the Nazis, you should have been the first to grab the slimmest opportunities and run into the woods to join the partisans."

"It isn't so simple, Vaitras, and you know it."

"Of course, but this is the chance you have to take. Your people were always persecuted, but somehow you always managed to get ahead? How did you do it?"

Aaron replied: "Hounded, laughed at, pushed around, we felt despised in your presence. You forced us to become clannish and stick with our own. That was the only place we felt safe. You denied us first class citizenship. You are the ones who estranged us from yourselves.

"Any action brings about a reaction. Your aim of putting us down, forced us up. When you are the underdog on a basketball team, you try that much harder to stay in the game.

"At the age of five a Jewish kid is taught that he is a born underdog and must learn more, and work harder, if he wants to succeed under your political system.

"You made it so hard and unbearable for a Jewish child to enter a government school that they were forced to form their own in the Yiddish language. Lithuanian, the official tongue, became his second language.

"Not using it at home or among his friends, he didn't learn to speak your language exactly like you, so you made his accent a laughing matter.

"You treated the Jew like a foreigner and yet you wanted him to respect you as a superior host who was allowing him to stay in his country. You tried to show your superiority by degrading him or by applying physical force. You were trying to convince him that you are superior, while you yourself knew you were not. You knew the Jew was educationally more advanced. Your hurt ego hurt even more.

"You saw Jews in business and you envied their income. The truth of the matter was that you couldn't and wouldn't work so hard, and such long hours.

"It is always easier to criticize than to understand people.

"We were no problem. We never needed nor did we ask for handouts from the government. We were self-sufficient and self-supporting. Your cities were built up with our taxes."

Vaitras nodded. A sign of agreement—or perhaps he just decided to give up for want of a good argument.

On a gloomy greyish day, Vaitras received an assignment to set a bomb under the police station. As they watched through binoculars, they could see that he was in difficulty. The plan was not working. A farmer, in a buggy, passing by, noticed him, and went straight to the police. Vaitras was captured and arrested. The safety of all partisans was at stake.

The time came for Aaron's first assignment: To execute Baltas, Chief of police, and to free Vaitras.

All was carefully planned. Aaron walked along a lonely road while the underground members covered him as far as they could without being spotted. If he were challenged, they would have to open fire. But they didn't expect any trouble as this narrow fourth-grade road was always deserted at this hour.

Dressed as an officer, Aaron walked with his head up, trying to resemble one. In his coat pocket he carried a loaded revolver which would be his answer to, "Your papers, please!" He headed toward the house of Baltas who was notorious for bringing in suspects to the small nearby court.

As Aaron approached his house, Baltas walked out. He was slim, in his thirties. He wore eyeglasses and had a rather mild face. He must have been expecting another secret order from his Nazi bosses. When he came closer to Aaron, the Nazi collaborator suspected that this was a

124

disguise. Something was wrong with the German uniform. It was wrinkled, oversized, and the boots were soiled. He saw an unshaven face, unusual for a German officer.

"Who are you?" Baltas asked with a trembling voice.

"Did you arrest Vaitras?" Aaron asked with a non-German accent. That gave him away completely. Baltas turned quickly and began to run toward his house. Aaron followed behind. Luckily there was no one inside except for a German Shepherd dog who jumped and grabbed Aaron by the sleeve, trying to reach for his throat. Aaron shoved the dog away and shot him with the revolver.

"Where is Vaitras?" he shouted nervously, holding the revolver at the chief's head.

"I didn't do anything to him. Somebody brought him in," Baltas pleaded.

"Where is he?"

"Don't shoot. I'll tell you. He is tied up to the kitchen stove. You can have him, but let me go."

"You are not going anywhere. Move!"

They walked into the kitchen. Bruised and dizzy, Vaitras lay on the floor against the wall, tied and gagged. At the sight of Aaron, he raised his head off the floor and quivered with relief.

"Untie his mouth, hands and feet," Aaron ordered Baltas.

Bewildered, Vaitras took a deep breath as soon as the two filthy handkerchiefs were taken from his mouth and nose.

"I can't get the cords off his feet," Baltas said. "They are too tight."

"You put them on, swine, now you can take 'em off."

"I need a knife to cut it loose."

"The only time you get a knife is to cut your own throat. Do you really expect me to trust you with a knife? Get going, I said!"

Baltas hurriedly began to pull on the cord knots with his fingernails shaking all over.

"Who tied you up, Vaitras?" asked Aaron.

"It was Baltas. He trapped me under the bridge and brought me here."

125

"I had to. I was ordered to do so. Hans Prager told me it's either Vaitras or me."

"He is lying. His Nazi bossman just promised him a promotion."

"He won't see another promotion if we can help it. When is your trial?"

"Tomorrow morning."

"They'll just have to get by without you. As soon as it gets dark we'll be on our way."

"What about me?" asked Baltas.

"What about you? You don't expect us to let you go free? Once a traitor, always a traitor. Where is your weapon?"

"In the closet."

Vaitras got up slowly. He gathered the gun in one hand, a belt with ammunition in the other.

"Go ahead, Vaitras, wash your forehead and put a towel over it. Let's see. It has almost stopped bleeding. How did it happen?"

"Baltas hit me a few times with his belt during the interrogation. I told him nothing. I just waited for death, and hoped it would be an easy one. I would have shot myself before getting captured, but I ran out of bullets."

"I t-told you," Baltas stuttered, "after the troop commandant found out Vaitras was hiding under the bridge, he told me that it was him or me. I was ordered to find out details. He wouldn't say a word. While I was tying him up, Vaitras slipped out and grabbed a knife. I got hold of his wrists and twisted it from his grasp. For that I was going to shoot him on the spot, but the boss ordered me to bring him alive into court tomorrow morning for questioning."

Vaitras said, "Baltas tried all kinds of tricks on me but they didn't work. He was enraged. Ordinarily the beating would have begun right there. This is a special squad of super-collaborationist police. But they had a fat catch of a dozen partisans from Briansk area, so he didn't get a chance to torture me much. The other men went through long and painful interrogations. Baltas was mean as hell.

126

The boys were tired and weak. He pushed and hit them. One of them fell. He kicked him a few times. Then he screamed at him: 'Get on your feet, you Bolshevick filth,' kicking and punching all the while. I could hear the screams, the moans, and cursing and roaring. The men being questioned were torn, bleeding wrecks. Baltas kept battering them. I felt sick to my stomach. I saw him walking back and forth swishing a riding crop. One of them was hit by Baltas every time he cried out. Then he hit one over the head and the blood coursed down his face into his eyes. He couldn't see. 'All you have to do is tell us where the rest of your Communist dogs are hiding,' Baltas said, 'and I'll stop this. You can make me stop it any time.'

"He put a pencil between the partisan's fingers and squeezed them together. Then he broke the fingers one by one. Everytime he did so he asked: 'Now what do you have to say?' After the man fainted he let me out. I thought I was going to faint from just watching his interrogation. The radio played "Deutschland Über Alles." He hit me with the weighted handle of the riding crop and said through gritted teeth: 'Tomorrow will be your turn, you louse!' He looked like one of the old horrors I saw in the movies when I was a youngster.

"The partisans were all jammed into a single cell. Inside it was filthy, with no beds, and cockroaches all over the floor.

"They decided to keep me separate over night." Vaitras looked out of the window, chewing on an end of a loaf of bread to which he helped himself. The village was covered with the dark of night. The court where he was to be led in the morning could hardly be seen.

"It's time to go," he said to Aaron.

"Ok. Baltas, you come along with us."

"Where are you taking me?" Baltas asked in a shaky voice.

He moved forward staring sideways with his beady eyes. At the first opportunity, he sharply sidestepped and tried to reach an axe hanging on the wall. Vaitras raised the revolver taken from Baltas to his face and pulled the trigger. Baltas rocked back, but did not fall. Then he fired again into his chest.

He put the gun in his pocket and said:

"Ok, he who digs a trap for someone falls in himself. Sorry Baltas, but I feel more sorry for your dog."

He and Aaron walked cautiously outside looking around into the pitch blackness. They could only see a few feet ahead. It was an ideal night for an escape. If they could only find their way back to the woods.

They turned in the direction of their camp on the other side of the valley across the narrow, walking path. Vaitras embraced Aaron, put his hand on his shoulder and said:

"I'm alive after all. I feel I'm living on borrowed time. I was hopeless until I heard you rush into the house and shout, 'Hands up, Baltas!' I didn't recognize your voice because I didn't expect you. It didn't sound like you. I guess you were excited. I sensed it was the voice of a partisan. Minutes before, I just hoped to die with as little torture as possible. I had no chance. I ran out of ammunition when they grabbed me. Before I got up Baltas kicked me real hard a couple of times in the stomach. My breath went and I collapsed.

"I told him I knew nothing and that I had nothing to say. I had not forgotten the lesson of our commander. . . . We are young, but we are brave and we fight for a just cause.

"You know, that did make a difference to me as to how I would die. It was either like a worthy partisan who did everything regardless of cost in order to protect his comrades, or like a traitorous coward without guts or morals."

"Didn't you ever think of escaping during the night?"

"I did. In the bright daytime I probably couldn't make it to our group from here anyway, but I had nothing to lose. I waited for dark. If I could only get up and move over to the kitchen, find a knife—well what's the use of talking about it. I'm free now. Man, it's like a dream."

Aaron moved his cap in a letter "z" formation and whistled do-re-mi, according to the agreed code. Several sentries who looked like shadows got up and rushed toward the returnees.

They were bear-hugged and kissed in European fashion. Vaitras felt warm tears rolling down his cheeks. He wiped them off quickly with his sleeve.

"What will they say?" he thought. Is this becoming to a partisan?

But a partisan is human too. And no one asked questions about the tears. They were together again. Who knew for how long? Vaitras was alive, and where there is life there is hope!

Everyone was too excited to go to sleep. Until late into the night he shared his horrors with his friends. They listened attentively to every word. Privately each prayed that things would work out for them, too, if they were ever caught.

Leaves were circling in the air, sideways, up and down, as if they couldn't seem to make up their minds where to land. Some went down and were tossed by the wind right back into the air to join thousands of others. They looked like butterflies powered in confused motion. Soon they were sprayed with a stinging rain. Aaron took out his calendar. It was Saturday. What had happened to the spirit of the Sabbath? How remote that was, and what was the use thinking about it?

12

THE PARTISANS FADED deeper and deeper into the woods. It was their island of refuge in a sea of tyranny. It was their bastion which they were determined to hold until death. And they preferred the higher areas where they could look down upon the enemy.

They mined bridges leading to their camp; they blocked tunnels. They prepared to stop trains and trucks. They would hit the Germans wherever they could, as hard as they could, as long as they could.

One night, as they lay asleep on the ground, they were awakened by a barrage of short-range artillery.

Faces were smeared with dust. Eyes, red-rimmed from lack of sleep, were covered with powder. Outnumbered and outgunned, and in spite of repeated calls from the Nazis to surrender, the partisans fought on.

Bullets whizzed over their heads and ripped around them. The encounter became more intense, more nerve-racking. Several fell, including the officer in charge. One partisan was wounded in the shoulder. It was one of their *dum-dum* bullets. He was hit in the shoulder and it ricocheted like an explosive bomb through his back.

Eventually the shooting from the Germans tapered down, then, stopped. It could be one of two things. Either they were waiting for re-enforcements or they were out of ammunition.

As the partisans debated, the Germans, as if they could read their minds, dashed toward the thick forest and disappeared.

Morale rose. Everyone felt like David fighting Goliath. The feeling of power was exhilarating!

But they didn't pursue the hated enemy. Their tactic was hit and run. They couldn't afford the luxury of following them and pressuring them. Not yet. . . .

With the arrival of the winter of 1943, the snow and rain converted the ground into a sea of mud. Armored units became paralyzed; offensive movements stopped.

When the Germans were stopped at the gates, the Red Command called for help from the partisans.

Guerrilla warfare was not new to the Russians. It was deeply embedded in their history. So when the Russian's capital was in danger they played on the sentiments of their people, living on both sides of the front line.

The Russian propaganda machine was most effective among the population during the German occupation. "The Germans attacked our country . . . they bombed our cities . . . they shot our people . . . our heroic partisans are fighting for you. Join in the struggle for freedom against the Nazis and their lackeys."

These statements encouraged the people behind the lines. Contrary to German claims, they learned that the Russian Army was not beaten yet. They learned they had stopped the murderous onslaught of the Germans and, most of all, that they were not alone in their fight against the Germans. Heartened by the news that their big brother was just on the other side, they lent more support to the partisans.

The frustrated Germans were slaughtering peasant families for offering the slightest sympathy to the partisans.

Many of those who were even in a small way involved in giving a starved partisan a piece of bread, or a place to warm up their frozen hands, earned German retaliation. To avoid it, they fled into the nearby woods and joined in the struggle against the invaders.

As the guerrilla ranks swelled, more help was given to them by the Red forces, some of which were stationed only several miles away.

Guerrilla raiders, and experts among all ranks and units, were retrained. The more dedicated and trusted partisans were the members of the Communist party.

German forces were sandwiched between the Soviet Army and the pro-Soviet guerrillas. Forced to retreat from a Russian offensive, German infantrymen escaped into the woods, only to be trapped and eliminated by the partisans.

Paralleling Russia's increased offensive, the partisans became more and more active. They cut communication wires which deprived the Nazi units from communication with the high brass command. Accustomed to blind obedience, the same troopers who had conquered one city after another became alarmed, and retreated when bullets began to pour in on them. They ran like mice from a flood.

Hitler had concentrated his main military punch against Moscow. He hoped to cut off the river Volga at Stalingrad. If this could materialize, he would be pretty much on his way to victory.

The Russian population, whether they liked Communism or not, had one thing in common with the partisans—they hated the Nazis. They all spoke Russian and communicated well. Noted for their friendliness and goodheartedness in normal times, the partisans easily found a spot in their compatriots' hearts.

The discipline was strict, the battles fierce. In small groups they took on small targets. They destroyed everything that was helping the German army. Germans and their local helpers who were called "enemies of the people," were shot without a pardon. No prisoners were taken. Selected captives were interrogated, then shot.

Ruthless in dealing with the invader and her Russian puppets, the partisans were just as severe in maintaining their own discipline. Leaving position, disobedience or disloyalty, was followed by immediate execution. Depending on their leader, the degree of the penalty varied from strict to stern.

In areas thinly occupied by German troops, the partisan movement swelled with occasional deserting policemen or escaped prisoners.

The Germans began to feel the pinch from the "bandits," as they were called, and began to employ more reconnaissance among their collaborators. Sellouts among the Russians in particular were very unpopular. They readily trapped themselves among the partisans with their inconsistencies. The partisans had a manual smuggled to them from the Red Army. It had a large number of specially designed questions. They didn't miss a trick. Based on the theory "a liar has a short memory," an impostor partisan once in their web of interrogation, couldn't get out alive.

Children sent to be "lost in the woods" by the Germans, to find the whereabouts of guerrillas, were stopped by the partisans. During the interrogation they turned out to be children of village leaders, encouraged to bring back information to the Nazis. When discovered, the children were taken home, and their whole family shot.

The wooded and hilly terrain with few roads created an ideal cover for partisan activities.

Through information gathered from the local population, small groups found each other and merged for security reasons.

In time, they became bolder and established a second front for the Red Army. Capitalizing on this development, Moscow began to train experts on guerrilla warfare among high echelon officers. These men were flown by light plane or helicopter to partisan units to supply them with leadership, propaganda manuals, information, radios, weapons, clothing and food. As they proved themselves reliable, the partisans began to enjoy more sophisticated equipment and, in some aspects, were treated like Red soldiers, although by law they were not allowed to join the Red Army.

The Red staff knew that nearly everyone can become a soldier, but few were cut out to be partisans. They realized the weight partisans carried behind the lines. They were needed too much where they were.

Encouraged, the partisans became more daring. Their

heroism inspired partisans in other countries. The Russian guerrillas became an example, and were idols to many. They had an advantage over the others. The Russian army had withstood the blitz. She was still unbeaten. Their support could always be counted on sooner or later.

This valued support made the partisans feel that they were not alone. They began to feel even more powerful.

The constant threat of partisans overrunning villages began to put a damper on the quislings. They felt more threatened.

When reports popped up about partisans taking over villages and even putting in their men to run it, Berlin ordered the formation of Jagdkommandos. Their goal was to encircle and destroy the "bandits." But these came a little too late and they were not a serious match for the strongly motivated partisans.

The partisans played their own game at home; in their own stadium. Competing on grounds as well known to them as their five fingers, and with Red military power on their side, they could not be stopped.

Even when the Germans trapped a band, the partisans would slug it out in real shooting fashion. The Germans seldom wiped them out, and German losses were heavy.

Harassment from the guerrillas coupled with the Russian offensive made their own German "superior Aryan blood," too precious to spill. They decided to substitute for it the blood of the inferior race, the blood of those Russian prisoners who volunteered to fight the Red Army. Those betrayers were led by Lieutenant General Andrei Andreevich Vlasov.

The Germans knew they had a puppet General on their hands. They encouraged him, and he jumped at the opportunity to remain a "General" and fight his former comrades. He became a pawn in the hands of the Nazis.

David and his unit were dug in at Stalingrad waiting for the big push. It was 1943. The Germans were besieged on several fronts and for the first time were forced to retreat.

Harassed by the partisans, they didn't know which way to run for cover.

The Red Army, aware of the Vlasovaites in that region, was ordered to fight and encircle the enemy. Thousands of turncoats fell into the hands of the Red Army.

Prisoners everywhere, in the thousands, were a strong indication of Hitler's forthcoming defeat. There were hungry, weak, frozen and wounded soldiers and officers, Germans and Hungarians, Rumanians and more Germans and Russians dressed in German uniforms. They were afraid to raise their heads, ashamed to look at anyone. They didn't reply to heckling; they were afraid to be recognized because they feared that their countrymen would show no mercy for their actions.

Prisoners, all separated according to their nationalities, went through a process of screening. No one looked as pale and as shaky as the Vlasovaites. They could see what was coming, and expected no miracles. On their faces was written: "Our adventure is over. Now come the consequences."

The news was beamed through all networks of the Soviet radio. Partisans like Aaron and soldiers like David heard the news alike. A date for a court trial was set, and groups of Red Army men were invited to watch the "Trial of Traitors."

David was one of twenty in his unit tapped on the shoulder to appear for the trial. It took place in a bullet-peppered, brick building. Inside, pictures of Stalin hovered over several tables set in one line next to each other, covered with a red cloth, facing several hundred chairs for Army spectators.

The jury walked in; everybody rose. A Colonel, two Majors, several Captains, and an interpreter, a Sergeant, took their seats. Their chests were covered with medals: The Hero of the Soviet Union, The Red Star, The Order of Lenin, For the Defense of Moscow. Stalin's picture was covered with all of these plus many others. A dozen of Vlasovaites were led into the room. They wore oversized German uniforms which looked like hand-me-downs. Pale and scared, they couldn't face their former compatriots.

They kept their eyes on the floor, occasionally throwing a look at the audience. There was no one they knew. In the Soviet Union there are two hundred million people. These were new faces. In the hour of questioning they admitted their names, previous units, and ranks.

The questioning lasted for several hours and toward the end, the turncoats became more weary. They were meek, their voices trembling.

Nikita Kula was the first one to be called to the stand. Bewildered and embittered he pulled his chin up and tried to look his best.

The first question came from a senior Lieutenant with judicial insignias on his epaulettes: "How did you happen to switch from Red to brown, meaning the uniform of the Nazis."

"*Nye ponimayu*—I don't understand."

"I'm asking you how did you get into that German uniform?"

"I was caught prisoner and drafted, Comrade Lieutenant."

"I'm not your comrade, so don't call me comrade. Secondly, don't waste time. Tell the truth."

"I'm telling the truth."

"Our intelligence service knows already too much to be fooled by a fool like you. Why did you volunteer?"

He paused for awhile.

"Tell me, I don't have a whole night for you."

"I was hungry, cold, miserable. One day General Vlasov came to our camp for a visit. He was dressed in a Russian uniform with his insignias missing. He tried to cheer us up: 'You don't have to rot in this camp; together with the victorious Germans we are going to drive the Communists out of power and free our homeland from them.' "

The prisoner's head sagged so low as if he was ready to faint, but soon he regained his composure and was ready to continue as the Lieutenant said:

"And then what happened? You thought it was a pretty good deal?"

136

"Yeh, I was not the only one. Thousands began to cheer and I thought maybe they had something."

"Something, what?" the angry Lieutenant snapped. "If thousands were to climb a cliff, would you do the same?"

"I guess not, but this was war."

"War?" the Russian officer shouted. "War against whom? Who came and occupied your country? Go ahead," he said covering a little cough with his hand. "Tell me where and how did you get captured."

"It was in Prague. General Bunyachenko explained that we were pulling out because our help was no longer needed."

"Your help? Whom were you helping? There were rumors that our tactics switched against the Germans."

"Did you shoot at the Germans?"

"We were ordered to shoot into a forest, but there was no one in sight."

"Were you told that you and your German friends were losing the war?"

"No. We were told that we only were switching to better positions."

"So your leaders didn't tell you that they were trying to save face and above all their dirty skins. And what happened then? Did you hear joyous shouts from your countrymen?

"We didn't."

"I'm sorry you didn't," the Lieutenant said sarcastically. "And what happened to the rest of your band?"

"We were told the army of Vlasov numbered around 50,000. When they saw how the Germans kept losing their grip on the front lines, there were whispers about making it across the Anglo-American lines. But on a foggy morning, when we were all surrounded by the Russian Army some, especially officers, committed suicide."

"Why didn't you?"

"I felt I was just a small screw in this machinery. I was misguided."

Replying to a question, why he had joined the Vlasov units, another replied; "I was cold and hungry. They promised. . . ."

137

"So for a piece of bread you volunteered to kill your brothers," a Major intercepted.

"You feel, you ought to be forgiven?"

"Yes."

"Well, this is up to the jury. Now go back to your seat."

A score of other Vlasovites were interrogated over a period of a week. They were accused of diversionary acts and terrorist activity against the Soviet Union and its people.

Most of them were sentenced to death by hanging.

A captain seated next to David said: "The sentence is stiff but fair. They surrendered to the Germans because they were cowards and they'll die as cowards."

The next day poles were erected about every hundred feet along the roads leading to the front lines. Hanging from them were blue-faced corpses in outsized German uniforms. Every post had a sign. "For the Traitors of the Motherland."

It served as a warning for the Red Army. It spelled: "Don't you try to do what they did if you don't want to hang along with them."

13

A SIGNAL OF HOPE began to zoom across the gloomy horizon. The partisans heard the sound of bombs exploding at ammunition dumps, railway stations and other strategic points of military importance.

The explosions sounded so good, Aaron wouldn't have traded them for the best orchestra. The famous Russian Katusha now made herself heard. A new, top-secret, long-distance cannon, placed on a heavy truck peeked out unsuspiciously from under a cover shaped like a boat. Villagers saw soldiers pass through the roads, and wondered where in the world they were heading with those "fishing boats" when the river was miles away.

The innocent looking truck-'n-boat had within it a piece of military magic. It could shoot up to twenty miles with deadly accuracy. The Katusha practically spat fire out of four openings. Its roar sounded beautiful, and the partisans jumped with joy every time they heard it.

The partisans shouted: "Davaj, let's go—hey, they are singing our song." Jammed into one foxhole, they put their arms around each other and sang.

In the evening they heard an almost endless cannonade. They named it the "Thunder of Freedom." They climbed trees and watched a real spectacle of fireworks.

This show, which introduced the real power to deal with Germany's oppression, made them so happy, they could hardly sleep from excitement. They called the show: "Color the SS Red and Green." Accompanied by an uproar, green rockets went up to light up the dark of night. Soon, the cannons followed with a few red flashes, and boxcars began to burn fiercely. An ammunition cave caught on fire and went crackling like peanuts under the shoes of a step dancer.

Soviet shells with their whining sound kept hitting targets more often and more accurately. Then a dozen Russian planes swooped down over the forest on their way to the railway station to continue the assault.

No one climbed down from the trees.

Those Russian steel birds looked beautiful. "What style, what speed!" one shouted. "And its loud, piercing sound is not bad either," another said.

"And those boys inside, I wish I could give their hands a shake, and kiss each finger separately," another added. "Hey, look at the one on the right, he just passed by without dropping a bomb. Must be a rookie, or maybe a girl!"

Direct hits began to find their marks and soon the sky was lit up. The Russian planes were having their field day.

Commander Bari tried to get in touch by radio, but it was no deal. The air was too thick with sound. "We'll have to wait until it's over before we can get sound," he said.

An hour later the shelling slowed down to a halt, but the area was still glittering from the fires and smoldering white and grey embers. It felt like the party was over; for the night anyway—until dawn at least. Perhaps they would see another shelling of the Germans. This time during the day. Nobody knew what would happen tomorrow. But one thing was crystal clear, the course of the war had changed. This time the Germans were on the run. It didn't take a military analyst to see it.

"*Vnimanie, vnimanie,*" the radio beamed. "Attention, attention." The partisans rushed over to the radio. "This is Pobeda. Over."

"This is unit Krasnaya Zviezda. We are on the outskirts of area 421. Can you hear me?"

"We can hear you well. Over."

"Get your weapons in top condition. Be ready to join us in a united front."

"We'll all be ready. Long live freedom!"

The joy of the partisans almost went out of control. A few moments were filled with hopping, bearhugging, kissing. Some had tears in their eyes.

How true is the saying, Aaron thought: "When we lose everything and we find just a part of it how happy we become."

The collaborators sweated nervously when the time of justice arrived. Like poisoned rats, the Ukrainian *polizai* nervously ran for cover to their German bosses.

Neither received much comfort since their confusion increased with every dropped bomb, every bullet. This change in the situation caught them by surprise.

They no longer had the time to look for new prisoners since this is what they themselves almost were. The Germans, who were in the habit of marching forward for their Fatherland, were suddenly forced to change their course and begin the retreat back to their Fatherland. Their heads, carried high during the time of their military successes, began to drop lower and lower, and every time a Russian airplane passed, their morale fell further. The Ukrainian puppets looked downhearted, and the Germans weren't about to console them. They had their own troubles.

A convoy of hundreds of German trucks, filled with military equipment and soldiers, tried to make it across a bridge. Several Russian planes swept down on them. The convoy stopped, and the Germans jumped off, sprinting in all directions, wishing they were worms who could crawl into the ground. A bomb dropped right on target. The bridge was blown up and with it their plans to escape.

As soon as darkness descended over the area, the Germans got to work restoring the bridge. It was several miles away from the partisan hideout.

The partisans sent out a flurry of bullets as a reminder that they were still around. They were doubtful the Germans were hit by them, but they were confident that they would hold up the rebuilding of the bridge.

The German propaganda machinery had been encouraging people from occupied territories to do more and better work for the Reich by using as their slogan "Work Makes Life Sweet."

"The Aryan master race," as they called themselves, who claimed to offer the world a "land to live in" found themselves struggling in a land to die in.

The soaring rate of casualties didn't discourage them. Compared to the massacres and the thousands of bodies they had seen, nothing could shock them any more.

At dusk several tanks were wrecked and smoldering. An armored car rumbled through as it tried to take away the wounded. It was the size of a large panel truck with bullet-proof armored boards and an open top.

The partisans had been re-inforced with more machine guns and ammunition which they had taken from a small arsenal. They had shot the guard whose last words were: "The *polizai* packed and fled leaving me on guard."

The growing and strengthened underground went after the remnants of the German column. There weren't many left. An attack in broad daylight proved that the partisans had overcome all fear. Through the countryside, they sneaked closer and closer to the location of the enemy, and at the agreed-upon signal, they poured in fire from two sides.

Germans were seen falling to the ground as they ran towards their armored car. Several grenades failed to set it on fire, but it was put out-of-order.

Railroads received Russian bombings, but now the partisans were right on hand to make sure no one was going to repair anything for the Germans. A locomotive tried to warm up with a few puffs of steam, but went no place. Again the partisans were right there to make sure.

The partisan movement came into its own and the Germans suffered. Little by little the partisans began to move out of the forest and occupied settlements with great caution. They began to patrol traffic from attics and roof tops.

The initiative started to shift in their favor and the local population began to show more respect toward the fighter who came from the underground onto higher and wider grounds.

Even those who didn't really look forward to the Russians' return couldn't help but look up to those boys who helped to support the Red offensive. In war, might makes right, and while it was might that the Germans possessed, it was the partisans who had the greater courage to fight them. They were heroic fighters, men of stature. They were hated by the Nazis, but the Nazis were now on their way out.

Five Russian planes zoomed by in a "V" formation and dropped bombs. It looked close, but it was at least five miles away. A forthcoming attack by the Reds was expected. Soon, the quiet countryside was interrupted by bursting artillery shells. The air was filled with earth, steel and concrete. From a distance several buildings could be seen ablaze. Flashes of tank guns began to stab into nearby area targets, followed by a hurricane of explosives.

The partisans began to cheer and holler like wild tribesmen, whistling and yelling to one another. This celebration was wild and joyous.

The show of force continued far into the night, but no one got tired watching it. No one went to sleep. It was a spectacular which couldn't be ignored. The red and yellow arrow flames coming out of the famous Katusha artillery kept the partisans' bodies warm in the chilly night.

It looked as if the Germans in that area were completely wiped out, and the Russians might arrive at any time.

The partisans couldn't hide their boyish manners any longer, nor control their emotions. They patted each other on the shoulder and shook hands. Some clapped and hopped for joy. A new slogan "Hitler kaput" swept the area.

A few chanted a prewar song, "If there is war tomorrow, we will defeat the enemy." Aaron was almost hysterical. He laughed until he cried. He jumped around so much his stomach began to ache.

They were finally exhausted from celebrating and ready

for sleep. But their rest didn't last long. They were awakened by voices: "Hey boys, hey! The Red Army is here. They are here!" Carrying automatic weapons, they walked in with an off-foot beat. It was more than just a parade; it was a march to victory.

They were dressed in khaki pants and wide knee-high over-sized boots and wore high-necked sloppy blouses. Their sweat-stained caps smelled badly, but to the partisans it smelled good. Introduced by microphone, they dashed to their liberators, full of smiles. The city of Achtyrka near Kharkov was full of Russian soldiers, Tartars, Armenians, Kazakhs and other colorful nationalities.

Red Army men handed out cigarettes. The partisans reciprocated with strawberries, tomatoes, or whatever they had on hand. It was one happy family.

A command to move on came. More handshakes, more smiles. Straight from the heart. They were real.

"Can we come along with you?" the partisans asked.

"Stay where you are, boys," a captain replied. "You'll get your directions. You won't stay jobless for long. There is plenty of work cut out for all of us. Just keep your cool and don't get trigger happy.

The partisans had no illusions about the Nazis. They knew about the horrors that had taken place under enemy rule. They had long ago come to terms with fear, living all through the war in anguished suspense.

The only males left anywhere were children under sixteen and men over fifty-five. Now, fleeing civilians who had cooperated with the Nazis clogged the roads. Their nightmarish stories about the Red Army's intention to kill every German and collaborator spread like an epidemic, filling many citizens with terror.

Not many preferred to dismiss it as propaganda. Alarming rumors began to pile up so high that the local administrations became more and more apprehensive. They stopped telling their people that victory was just around the corner, and switched to reassurance. The Wehrmacht, they told the people, is only pulling back temporarily, to improve strategic positions. They'll be back.

144

The joy of an oncoming peace for those who had re-
sisted was marred by condemned men hanging from the
gallows along the road. It was depressing, and took the
joy out of spring. "Who are these men?" a woman asked.

"I don't know any of them. We were told that they
were wounded partisans. They were captured and hung. A
sign hanging over one body, said in Ukrainian: "I'm a
filthy Communist."

"Where can we get a ladder that high to take them
down?"

"The nearest fire department is about twenty miles
from here."

A group of partisans called a partisan unit stationed
in the area and asked if it was possible to bring on the fire
engines.

They then picked out two of the strongest ladders and
tied them tightly together. The lightest in weight stepped
up while a dozen formed a human wall below. With a knife
he cut off each man one by one, seven of them altogether.

At the foot of a river, where the ground is soft and
lovely, the dead fighters were buried. A sign was stuck
in the ground, and on it was marked: "Glory to the seven
unknown partisan heroes." A few flowers were gently put
in the ground before the night darkened the blue-white sky.

At dawn many more flowers were seen. Where had they
come from? The villagers had taken fresh flowers right out
of their gardens and placed them there, in sympathy for the
young lives who had dared refuse to obey the orders of their
occupying oppressors.

In one place, women tractor operators were taking a
rest while others were pitching hay. A mounted shepherd
drove his charges on a collective farm.

Two boys climbed on a partition rail and amused themselves with the peasant's game of balancing. Inside, an
elderly farmer lit a cigarette and took a long pull while
computing a sale on an abacus.

The soft air and the flowering fields brought on a holiday
mood. Young teens strolled through the sandy streets, sing-

145

ing to guitars with a beauty that hinted at the beginning of a new era.

With spring in the air, the drab little houses began to show some color. The grass was looking greener. The air smelled more pleasant; birds sang more beautifully, and even the hogs sounded more agreeable and friendly.

Paper strips, which had been pasted on windows to prevent the glass from shattering during the air raids, were stripped off. Windows were thrown open and flower pots watered. A gorgeous tulip burst open. It looked as if it were trying to say, "Just color me any shade of life."

A little sailboat was bending to the wind, and crows were swirling around endlessly.

Children were running in and out of the air raid shelters. To them, today was the day for fun, for play. On their smiling faces, the word "happiness" could be read. It was their fortune, their world. A new world in which there would be time to listen and time to talk; and time to take inventory of the loss of lives.

But above all, there would be an atmosphere in which to love and to be loved. Oh, how people would need it, to heal the wounds caused by this tragedy! The damage done to man could never be repaired; nevertheless, people looked for hope, for consolation. Like broken branches, people had been removed from their family tree.

But all of this would heal! People merge, unite, marry. New roots are needed to get the tree to grow. New books would be needed to get culture to flourish. Life would bloom again.

While Aaron reviewed all this in his mind, he saw precious human beings waiting in a stuffy train depot. They were sharing crumbs of bread, some fruit, and a home-made drink called *kvaas*. As he stared at this revived humanity, he could see it bloom along with the friendly surroundings.

Soon, the partisans were notified to be on the alert. An order came to camouflage themselves with leafy branches, and to get ready to wade across a shallow river where small pockets of Germans were still hiding. From a secret source they learned that the enemy was housed at the home of a Russian collaborator nicknamed, Uncle Fritzovicz.

The object was to blast them out of his farmhouse.

By early dawn the mission was successfully completed. The Germans were the first to surrender by waving a white towel from a half-open window. Questioned, they readily admitted their Ukrainian host's whereabouts. He lay quietly under his bed hoping the partisans would miss him. They didn't.

Watching the partisans' rifles trained on him he pleaded:

"Please, brothers!"

"Don't you call us brothers."

"But have mercy on me, I'm just an innocent farmer."

"A farmer you are, but you're not innocent. You tried to sell to the Germans our country for which so many of our people shed their blood. Now you'll pay with your blood."

"But please. . . ." One bullet stifled his voice. The Germans looked on without remorse. It was obvious that all they cared about was saving their own skins. Unable to understand the conversation in Russian, they sensed that the man was shot for collaborating with them.

The five captured Germans awaited the same fate. The partisans were undecided. A call on a radio unit received a prompt reply: "The Red Army will be there at any hour. Keep them under arrest. We'll need information from them."

The Germans looked at their mortally wounded ally with indifference. Aaron felt like calling him the names he deserved, but the words stuck in his throat.

It was now obvious to the local population that the partisans were in full command. The time came for "squaring old debts," and mobs roamed the area looking for revenge. Barefoot teenagers smashed store windows, cursing the owners loudly.

A youngster pushed himself through the crowd with an axe and cracked open the wooden door of a store. The mob jammed inside and rushed to the shelves. In a jiffy all bottles were grabbed up and corks started to pop. A comical scene followed.

A man with a bottle in his hand climbed through a window. The window was broken, and pieces of glass stuck out like razors. He was cut and bleeding. He touched his head with his hand and wiped the blood off. Another sip of vodka and there he was inside the dress shop. He put on a dress, then tried on a hat in the mirror. The scene was hilariously funny and everyone burst into loud laughter.

The shrieking mob became more bold and arrogant as the wines and vodka took effect.

The old Burgermeister was dragged out of his house and forced to march with broom in hand, and a broken pail over his head. *Raz, dwa, tri*, several youngsters counted excitedly in a chorus. *"Davai, davai,* let's go, let's go," the bystanders hollered.

The mob showed approval of this action by applauding and shouting sarcastically—"Bravo, there marches our superior Nazi, make room for royalty, folks, make more room. Hey Vanka, pull in your stomach and stand at attention. Can't you see the Burgermeister is marching by."

"Yes, how about that!" Vanka replied.

He took the empty bottle by its neck and banged it on the pail over the former chief's head. The bottle broke and the shock almost swept the Burgermeister off his feet.

"Once more! Again!" someone hollered.

"Kill him, kill him!" people shouted. Soon he was dumped to the ground and trampled to death.

As the night began to close in, the crowd began to dwindle. But those who were enjoying the intoxication didn't give up.

"Let's get them all—the sons of whores."

"Hey, Paluchin . . . Panczyk where are you? Come out in the open and may the best man win. Let's see you."

"We want the cowards!"

"We want the cowards!" they chanted. But Paluchin, Panchik and other former administrators were not available for the challenge. The cowards had escaped. They were not ready to face the music.

A few more broken windows and the dark night swallowed the last shouts.

The next morning the Russian tanks rolled in. At the sight of those rattling steel turtles, a column of chickens and geese scrambled to the side. The streets began to swell with people. They were curious to see the men with whom they shared the good and the bad for most of their lives. It was quite awhile since they had last seen Russian soldiers dressed in the "old" uniforms, "the way they used to be." They were dressed in green with a star on the cap, a star on the belt, a star on each button. Some wore medals shaped as stars. They had stars all over.

Strangers embraced and girls became glued to the saluting partisans like flies to honey. The tanks stopped before the cheering people.

Excitement was everywhere. Girls were singing and clapping hands while boys hopped up and down doing their famous *tshastushki*.

One woman could not stop crying. . . .

The next day radios from Russian mobile units continuously beamed an announcement: "All partisans of this region are to attend a meeting at City Hall."

At the arranged time several hundred came from all directions by foot, horse, or on bicycles captured from the Wehrmacht. Most were in their twenties, unshaven, dressed in civilian clothing. Several were dressed in Red Army coats and German boots. About two dozen female partisans could be spotted among them. They had lived a hard man's life for so long that many looked like men; the same coat, same boots, same cap. They even walked like men.

Due to communication and transportation difficulties the meeting started two hours late. A five-man delegation from the Red Army was on hand. They took seats at the head table next to the obvious leaders of the partisan units: four men and a woman dressed modestly just like any other partisan.

They sat erect, all with a serious look in their eyes. A Captain, the spokesman for the Army, began with an opening speech.

149

"Comrades, partisans: In the name of the glorious Soviet Army I have the privilege to greet you and congratulate you on your great job. Your unmatched fight helped us to rout the Nazi beast. Now we are united for good, and together with the rest of our Soviet people we'll pursue the Nazis until final victory."

"—Long live the Soviet Union!"

"—Long live the Soviet People!"

"—Long live our great Father, Comrade Stalin!"

"—Long live the unbeaten Red Army!"

"—Long live the men without fear, our heroic partisans!"

They all got up and applauded.

A spokesman for the underground fighters got up and took equal time.

"Comrades, there is no greater thrill for me than to acknowledge the defeat of Nazism. The blood of our comrades wasn't spilled in vain. Their spirit is right here with us."

"From the beginning of the war we knew that we were on the right side, fighting for a just cause. And now, more than ever, we are convinced of it."

"Down with Nazism!"

"Down with their lackeys!"

"Long live Soviet leadership!"

"Long live the iron-tough Red Army!"

A partisan girl rose and handed the Captain a bouquet of flowers. As he shook her hand, she kissed him on the cheek. His face turned red like a blushing, shy country boy, and said: "Now! That is something I didn't expect. It wasn't part of my duty, but I'm not going to protest. I'll accept it as an extra bonus directed to all my army comrades."

"And now," he said becoming more serious, "I'll ask every partisan starting from the left of the first row to come up to this table." A red, white and green ribbon was pinned to each one of the fighters, and with a modest handshake they returned to their seats.

As the ceremony ended, both doors opened wide and Red Army men began to bring in cases of wine and cakes.

"A toast, *za svobodu*—for freedom," was heard. Other toasts were drowned out by voices which grew louder as the consumption of wine increased. *"Vnimanie!* Attention!" The Captain tried to outshout the noisy crowd. "Everybody goes back to his unit. You will be advised of your future assignments."

While the Red Army was pushing toward Berlin for the final phase of the war, the partisans were asked to continue with their service, but now in a different capacity; to strengthen the hold on the recaptured territories, to secure the areas from the "enemies of the people," meaning, basically, the Ukrainian turncoats who began to sneak back home.

And in spite of the tremendous casualties of the war in which the Russians suffered seventeen million killed, ten of whom were civilians, the Soviets did not collapse. Soviet military leadership and the quality of its troops improved.

Women who had learned in peacetime to do most of the men's jobs, became an important source in filling the homefront jobs in almost all walks of life. They played an important role in factories where new T-34 tanks were hurriedly built as replacements for the many lost in the blitz. Also, captured German vehicles were quickly repaired and a Red Star was painted over the black and white cross, and then it was rolled back to the front lines to pursue the enemy. In 1942, at Stalingrad, Hitler made his big mistake when he thought he could do better than Napoleon had done thirty years before.

A merciless winter came early and it caught the Nazis in their underwear, as the Russians said. Numb with cold and dazed by constant defeat under the weight of the Red offensive, they became politically disorganized and physically paralyzed.

Field Marshall Paulus surrendered along with his trapped army. From there on the Russians hardly stopped pushing forward.

Along with the rest of the partisans, Aaron volunteered to stay on the Security Force. For several months he worked in the Housing Department. Houses, which are government

151

property under the socialist system, were distributed according to the size of the family and position held.

There were better homes available, left by the collaborators. Aaron assigned those to the partisans.

There was a special treat announced on the local news: The Army Song and Dance Assembly was coming to entertain them. It was free, too. So, the price being right, many customers were expected. The floor of the City Hall was scrubbed clean of the German boot marks. Several Studebaker trucks marked, "Made in the USA," with a big red star on the door pulled up. Black and red letters painted on white sheets spelled:

Glory to the Red Army.

Long live the partisan movement.

Death to the fascist beast.

There was a series of caricatures showing the German soldier running in panic with his pants on fire while a Russian collaborator held on to his boot, kissing it.

A man was hanging from the gallows, while an amused SS tells his superior officer, "He just wouldn't tip his hat for me."

There were so many more that the marred walls were almost covered.

People began to arrive hours early. It was a sort of holiday around the City Hall because that's where the action was. A radio installed in front of the part brick, part wood building sent out songs about a boy longing for his girl, or a mother waiting for her son to return home after the victory. There were surprisingly few military songs. The prewar song about the Katusha, Russia's pride secret weapon, was picked up.

People were dressed in their best clothing. Some had a patch here and there, but they were clean. A wiry old man fingered his cactus-like hair upward and put his cap on, scratching his beard.

The hall began to fill up. On the first seat sat a farm woman. She was so fat and clumsy it was hard to tell whether she was sitting or standing up. Her two little girls were sitting on either side of her. Out of a brownish *ba-*

bushka she took two hard candies and stuck one in each mouth. For herself, she pulled out a long, fresh, green cucumber and wiped it off on her dress, bit into the edge and spit it out, chewing up the rest of it in a few seconds.

Behind her, as several partisans stood up to wave to a friend, a woman lost her balance and fell to the floor.

"Prosti mamasha, sorry mama."

"Why don't you sit like others do?" she said, provoked, picking up her rolling apples off the floor.

But she wasn't really angry. Somehow, a jolly mood prevailed throughout the celebration. An atmosphere of the approaching end-of-war hung in the air.

14

DAVID'S LETTER never reached Natasha.

Her village was overrun by the Germans a few days after he left. The lumber yard where she worked was razed by a bomb. It happened at night while she was alone in her home. She was awakened by a loud explosion and saw the wreckage when she went to work the next morning. Enemy troops were there already. Parked on the main street, they began to establish a foothold in the small community.

Smoke smoldered from a statue of Lenin, and its head lay at its base. Soon the population found the rest of the town's statues, including the ones of Stalin and Lenin, headless. People associated with the Communist party got the message.

A man climbed atop a fire ladder. On his arm he wore a band marked "National-Ukraine Militia." In both hands he kept a massive sledge hammer and chipped away at the over-sized Stalin face. The hammer bounced off the steel bronzed material as if it was made of rubber. Finally, after his effort to "behead" Stalin failed, he climbed down and the fire truck left. Police ordered all onlookers to move to the other side of the river. Sticks of dynamite were put around the statue and powerful explosions erupted, breaking nearby window panes. The statue almost collapsed.

The militia was busy making street arrests of Red suspects. People dispersed and went home, nodding and shaking their heads.

Natasha recognized one of the militiamen. It was Nikolai Solenko. He looked pale and angry, his face hungry for revenge. He showed rudeness towards his countrymen, pushing them and calling them filthy names.

Natasha recalled how he had been put in jail less than a year ago. He was the city's misfit and an accomplice in many crimes.

This was his chance to take it out on others. They hadn't done anything wrong to him, but that didn't matter. He chased people screaming: "Who else is a Red? I'm going to turn him blue and yellow." He hit everyone he suspected of being a communist. Then he grabbed a crippled shoemaker, Michael Taskaev, by the collar.

"Hey! You look like a Red rat to me."

"Please, brother," Michael pleaded. "I'm not a communist, I'm an anti-communist."

Hearing that Solenko replied: "I don't care what kind of a communist you are," and hit him twice over the head. This was all Natasha could bear. She left in agony as if she herself had received those two blows over the head, and when she was deep enough in the crowd she screamed out with all her might, "Beast!"

Solenko heard it, and looked around, but was unable to find out who said it.

Out of a job, Natasha went to City Hall. There, to her astonishment, she saw posters printed in Ukrainian, calling for loyalty to the German army.

Several office jobs were offered in a nearby city. Being all alone she picked up her few belongings and walked the few kilometers. She learned of a job in a police station. She was a little hesitant, but then decided to take it since "no one would get hurt by her pen and pencil."

Natasha soon learned that her innocent pencil indirectly pointed out some of her neighbors, and her pen doomed her compatriots.

She kept her eyes open and her mouth shut. She learned of many being doomed. After being sworn in under strict secrecy, she became a figure in the militia. She began losing hours of sleep and kept thinking of ways of escaping. It wasn't simple. There was a harsh penalty for such action.

There were rumors flying around about a partisan camp in the area, but she didn't have the vaguest idea where it might be. Without showing a hint of suspicion, Natasha tried to find out about the location from her boss, Mikhail Zayenko.

Zayenko, married and father of four, mistook her curiosity. He imagined that she was flirting with him. He smiled when she talked to him, and practically melted when she looked into his eyes. He began to place more trust in her and to reveal top secrets.

He hoped to gain her affection by confiding in her.

On several occasions he made advances to her, but was repulsed. He then tried to feed her with more news, hoping to soften her up, but was unsuccessful.

On the first anniversary of the occupation by the German troops, Natasha had an opportunity to meet the brass of the Ukrainian Militia. The "First Anniversary of Liberation of the Ukraine" took place in the small wooden building of the City Hall.

Two dozen militia men squeezed into the small room and occupied several rows of benches. In front, three chairs were reserved for dignitaries—the Gestapo bosses.

Zayenko was standing at the entrance, playing host. His buttons were glittering and his boots shining. His hair, moist with tea from the Samovar, was combed upward. With his hands behind his back and chin forward, he paced, nervously awaiting his German dignitaries.

Suddenly, like an eagle scout, he straightened up and called for everyone to stand at attention.

He looked like a cheap lackey as he walked sideways, one step ahead, showing the Germans to their seats. With a false smile on his face, and a cringing bow, he looked as if he were out for a tip.

He rose to speak to those gathered, and began with a blessing and special thanks to the German army for liberating his country from the "communist oppressor."

"Now," he went on, "Ukraine is free. We are going to get rid of the communal farms. We are going to take the art out of the churches and put it where it belongs, and bring the people back into the churches so they can pray for bigger victories for the brotherly German army; for the total destruction of the Red plague and a new national Ukraine."

During his speech Zayenko made sure to throw a few forceful smiles in the direction of the three front chairs with the three Gestapo men who couldn't care less. They were bored and were just waiting for their puppet chief to finish so they could go back to their *frauleins*, the Ukrainian girls. Numerous girls virtually offered themselves to the Germans, who were portrayed to them by the quislings, as their liberators. When Zayenko finished mumbling his speech, he was the first one to open the door for the departing Germans.

Natasha took a violent distaste to him. She couldn't look him in the eyes. "He is the one I detest most," she thought.

Immodestly, he asked her the next day what she thought of his speech. "How did I look?"

"You looked like a *shmata*, a rag. You only showed the Germans your inferiority and helped them to believe that they were superior," she burst out in anger, and walked away.

He struck her. "How dare you talk to me like a Bolshevik Jew? How would you like to appear in one of my courts and be put in jail?"

She looked at him and spat: "And how do you like being a mat for your Gestapo boss? Do you enjoy being kicked by him and hearing him say: 'Turn around, you bum, I have seen enough of this dirty side of you!'"

Stunned, Zayenko stood speechless for a moment. But soon overcoming the initial shock, he hollered: "Get out, you Red broad, out of here!"

Natasha grabbed her jacket, her face burning, and hurriedly left the police office. She didn't stop for a minute

157

to think of her future. But very soon she would have to consider what to do. She was in a dangerous position.

Where now? It seemed to her that the only way for her to save her dignity and escape harsh punishment would be to join the underground. It was a Saturday afternoon. She had had a whole night to think about it and a full Sunday to make it to the woods. The key question was, in which direction? The woods stretched for kilometers.

As she got busy in her garden picking her favorite fist-sized tomatoes, she kept her eyes open. Zayenko might send one of his *polizai* to get her. Carefully, she moved with her basket to the nearest potato crops which bordered the thick forest. There she could disappear at the first sight of Zayenko or his men, if she had to.

She was going to go deep into the woods and try to find some clue that might lead her to the partisans. But the time was not right. Caught by the *polizai*, she would be accused of trying to escape to the partisans and this would give Zayenko a perfect excuse for her execution. She decided to wait and to get an early start in the morning. No one could be suspected or accused for "picking berries on a Sunday."

Soon, it turned darker and cooler. She ran into her house, took her *perina* quilt, pillow and blanket, and down she rushed into the thick woods to stay overnight.

Never did she dream so much. It seemed like it lasted all night. She saw herself entering partisan territory among big, full trees. To greet her there was David himself. He was dressed in the gray jacket she had given him before he left her house, khaki pants, brown army shoes and green cloth leg wrappers called *obmiotki*. He grinned with his pearl-white teeth showing. Above the upper shirt, in a V-shape, his thick hair showed. This was the same comforting chest to which she clung the night before he had left. She was so happy to find a decent human being. She felt newborn, holding on to David with both hands until she awoke with her pillow in her arms.

Early in the morning, with her basketful of bread and tomatoes, she went deeper into the woods. Several hundred

158

feet seemed like miles. She walked straight in one direction. Should she have no results, she would know how to return to her home if she wished. She walked at a steady pace for over an hour and decided to sit down and have a bite to eat.

The partisan's observation point way up in a high tree was located on a hill. It overlooked the area leading towards the forest in which the partisan group camped. A guard noticed Natasha entering the forest. At that moment, he didn't find it too unusual, since on Sundays farmers entered several hundred feet deep into the woods to pick berries. With a basket on her arm, Natasha didn't look suspicious. But she was seen moving steadily deeper and deeper into the woods without stopping. When she had crossed half way toward the camp, the guard watching on top of the tree, began to follow her closer through his field glasses. He asked a comrade on guard to inform their leader about a girl moving toward partisan territory.

Soon their leader, Igor, came along with Nina, the only girl partisan.

"Comrade Nina, watch for a girl in her twenties walking by herself from the northeast. For the last twenty minutes she has walked in our direction. Now she is straining away slightly eastward. She looks constantly in all directions as if she is trying to find something.

"Nina, walk in the west and south direction. Keep going and I'll follow you about ten feet behind."

The command followed: "Nina can you hear me? You are about 250 feet from the suspect. Slow down. The girl is walking straight towards you . . . 150 feet divides you from her, get behind the first wide tree and stay there. Let her come closer to you. Within ten to twenty feet, walk casually toward her and ask her how to get out of these woods, into the village. Tell her you are lost."

Natasha saw this strange woman walking directly toward her.

"*Privit podruha,*" Nina greeted Natasha in Ukrainian. It was not an expression used in the local dialect, so Natasha knew that this woman was an outsider. "Aren't you lost?"

"I hope not," replied Natasha, "I started by picking strawberries, then I decided to explore the woods. I've lived here all my life and never really saw the true beauty."

"Strawberries?" Nina said leaning over in an effort to look into her basket. "But you don't have a single strawberry. What are you really looking for?"

"I guess I'm just enjoying the beauty of nature and the birds," Natasha said, observing this stranger in old wrinkled clothing covered with a man's jacket, her hand in a bulging pocket.

"*Harno, divka*, Ok girl," Nina said. "Now tell us the truth." The man who was following Nina had walked up to them. He stood near, and he looked fierce.

"And who are you two anyway?"

"Do we look like a pair of German lakeys?"

"Then you must be partisans. Before I tell you any more take me to your camp."

"We are partisans, but we can't show you our camp. Not before we find out who you are and what you are up to."

Natasha's voice began to tremble.

"Let's sit down and talk." She took out a few fresh tomatoes and bread and shared them with the two strangers.

"I have been working in a police office. I took the job because I didn't see any harm in pushing a pencil; it's better than pulling a trigger, you know. But soon I found out that my job helped the *polizai* and Gestapo to commit crimes against many innocent people."

"So you came to us," Nina said. "What can we do for you?"

"I came here to find out what I can do for you."

The two partisans took a look at each other. They liked the way she had phrased it.

"A girl like you can do lots for us. But first tell us some more. Why did you wait so long to make your decision?"

"In the few months with the *polizai* and Gestapo I

160

learned a few things; *ony skatyny*, they are animals of the worst sort."

"*Pravda*, it's true," the man said, "but how do we know that if we take you in, you won't change your mind and run away at night to report on us?"

"How do you trust your other members?" asked Natasha.

"They're with us from the beginning of the war. None of them has been working for the other side. Some came to us with weapons, the rest proved themselves."

"How can I prove myself?"

"Now you are talking. Tell us who is your Gestapo chief?"

"Hans Prager."

"Right. How does he look?"

"He is about thirty-five, tall, skinny with a bent upper lip."

"Right. Now, you want to prove yourself to us? He comes in on Monday afternoon. Go back, and tomorrow bring him to us."

"But how?"

"I'll tell you how. When he comes, tell him you feel sick and ask him if he wouldn't mind driving you home on his motorcycle. On the way tell him you feel all right . . . it must have been fresh air that you needed.

"Ask him if he would mind stopping in the forest for a little rest. Then sit with him on the back seat, hold close to him and press tight against his body. Tell him that you always wanted to be with him and that you faked your illness just to be with him. Give him a hint that you mean business.

"Make sure to enter the woods with him while it is still light, so we can locate you. Talk to him, tease him, without giving in. If he tries to subdue you say, 'please, not on our first date. What kind of a girl do you think I am?' Stall as much as you can. We'll be there in force to trap him. If you do it, that will be your partisan membership card."

Natasha listened intensely, then repeated it. "*Harno, do pobaczinia*—a deal. I'll see you again."

"We'll count on you. If you betray us, we'll catch up with you sooner or later."

The leader looked at his compass and said:

"Now follow me. Keep going straight ahead and you'll be back in your village. Don't forget to pick some berries on the way so people will believe you went to pick them."

Natasha burst into nervous laughter and disappeared between the trees.

She felt the pounding of her heart when she found the door of her house half open. Inside was Zayenko trying to open a heavy drawer, filled with books and papers.

"And just what do you think you are doing, breaking into my house? You are my boss at work, not in my house. Get out!"

"I'm your boss. I'm going to find out who my employees are."

"It's none of your dirty business."

"Oh, yes it is. After what you said yesterday at work I'm going to look into it and check your loyalty. Don't you worry, you Red tomato, I'll take care of you—in jail."

"Yesterday I felt sick," she said turning pale. "Don't you ever say harsh things when you don't feel well? I consider you my friend. How can I believe you when you say you love me."

Zayenko walked slowly over to the bench and sat down. For a while he looked at the floor, as if he was trying to find the right answer.

"Prostij, milka—forgive me, my dear. Perhaps I'm too harsh with you, but maybe it is because I didn't expect to hear those words from you. Let's make up."

She moved away from him, as he attempted to embrace her.

"Don't, Zayenko, I'm having my period and I still feel sick."

"Then why didn't you stay home? Where have you been?"

"I went to the forest to pick a few strawberries," she said handing him the basket.

"Where were you? Across the fields? Partisans are there somewhere. Did you see any?" asked Zayenko.

162

"I didn't see anything. How come you never warned me? They may come out at night and shoot me. Where are they?" she said in a terrified voice.

"We don't know exactly where."

"Why don't you find them?"

"Our local force is too small to trap them."

"What about the Gestapo?"

"They tell us to keep them inside the woods where they'll starve or freeze to death. I'll see you in the morning, Natasha, and don't worry about those bandits."

He tried to embrace her but she quickly moved away and said: "Please Zayenko, not today, but I'll be all right in a few days."

He left, and Natasha quickly locked the door. So far she had played her part well—she thought.

Tomorrow is another day; a big one for her!

She went to bed and planned all night. What if Prager doesn't show up? What if he gets sick or transferred? The partisans will think that I came to find out where they are located and then betray them.

What if I get him to come with me in the woods and he rapes me under gunpoint? How can I keep him there till they come? . . . What if he gets suspicious and decides to shoot me for it? What if he won't come along with me? Maybe he has a date for tomorrow afternoon with another girl? I just can't let the partisans down. This is my only chance to prove my dedication to their cause.

The thought of switching from an unjust to a just cause made the tension somewhat easier, yet Natasha did not fall asleep until well into the late hours of the night.

Monday morning was dewy. The air looked greyish, as if waiting to rain.

She had a cup of tea with *prikuska*, a lump of sugar. She put on her best dress and left for work. On her way, hundreds of thoughts went through her head. She felt uneasy, nervous; and tried to console herself. "Things usually turn out better than we expect," her father used to say. Her heart pounded as she opened the door of the militia building.

"Dobre utro," Zayenko greeted her at the entrance. "How do you feel today?"

"Still a little sick, but I'll be all right tomorrow."

As he put his hand on her shoulder a cold shiver went through her body.

She tried to memorize a new Gestapo order she was typing as an extra bonus for her new comrades.

The telephone rang. Zayenko picked up the receiver.

"I'll be right there," he said in an excited voice.

He ran into the next room and hollered: "Get your arms and line up boys. Outside!"

He grabbed his *polizai* cap, a rifle, and ran after them.

I wonder who is going to die this time? Natasha asked herself.

An hour later they returned. Zayenko was not among them. The five *polizai* lay on benches placed along the walls, like lions fattened after a feast. Their faces were white like sheets and their eyes popped like frogs'.

Natasha was eager to find out about what had happened. She called Petrylo. He, she thought, was most likely to tell her the truth.

"Petrylo, I need your help with the table. One of its legs is shaky."

He got off the bench trying to straighten himself. He got a hammer, a few nails and went to work.

"Tell me Petrylo, where is Zayenko?"

"Just about an hour ago he was tipped off about a partisan hiding in Voronkos' house. As we approached, the partisan ran out of the house. He hid under a bridge and shot it out. When the partisan ran out of bullets, Zayenko grabbed him by his hair and dunked his face ten times into the river. The man almost drowned. Then he hit him until he fell unconscious. He made me shoot the Voronkos, all seven of them. Their screams and cries will remain with me forever. It's tragic that we are destroying our own people. Such good people like the Voronkos, honest, hardworking people. They loved everybody."

"Tell me, Petrylo, how did you ever get into the *polizai?*"

164

"I had no work. Zayenko told me my job would be to keep law and order. Being a lawful man who likes order, I accepted his offer. In the beginning I delivered reports and messages to homes. Now I'm ordered to kill, and am faced with shooting somebody or being shot myself. That doesn't give me much choice, does it? I find myself between one death and another. But no matter how you look at it, it's our own people we are shooting every day."

"If you don't like your job, why don't you quit it?" Natasha asked.

"I asked Zayenko to be relieved. He said, never! Once a *polizai*, you'll remain one till we defeat the Reds, he said. I guess there is too much a *polizai* knows to be let off the hook."

Natasha had gone to school with him. She knew his nature well. He was always kind and wouldn't hurt anyone. She was tempted to confide in him and perhaps give him a hint as to how he might escape in the woods, but she didn't dare. That could torpedo her own plan.

"Do you know if Prager is coming today?" she asked.

"Yes, he should be here today, in an hour or so."

The roar of a motorbike acknowledged his arrival. He walked into the office with a salute, *"Heil Hitler."*

"Wo ist Zayenko?" he asked Natasha.

"You'll have to ask his men in the next room."

"How long are you going to stay here, Herr Prager?" she asked with a charming smile.

"Just an hour or so. Why are you asking, *libchen?*"

"Would you like to take me home, I have a slight headache?"

"I will be back for you around six o'clock, *shatzchen.*"

"Thank you, Herr Prager. I'll be through with my work by then."

The wall clock just rang six, when Prager came for Natasha.

"Ready, Fraulein Natasha?"

They walked out of the building. The motorbike was all shining, in tip-top shape. She sat behind him, and it took off.

"Where is your house?" he asked.

"Take the road to your right. It won't be far. I hope I'm not inconveniencing you."

"No, I have the whole evening to myself."

"You know what, Herr Prager, my head begins to feel better. The fresh air does wonders for me. Would you care to pull over to the side of the forest where we can have a chat."

"Your wish is my command, *Meine gnadige* Fraulein."

She took his arm and led him several feet inside the forest, behind a thick bush, just enough not to be seen by outsiders. Her wooing began to affect his ego. He grabbed her and pulled her over on top of him. As she was struggling out of his arms, several partisans jumped him and bundled him up like a baby.

"Halt! Who are they? Help me, Natasha! What is going on? *Krutze fixe!*"

Before he even saw the men, his revolver was taken and he was tied and gagged. The partisan anchor man took a long look from behind the bush and, apparently satisfied with the way it turned out, said:

"We are in the clear. Let's move."

When they reached the camp, Bari said:

"Untie him and take his female companion away."

"Companion?" Prager murmured.

"Why don't you just call her your agent, that cheapie. . . . I should have known better than fall for it. A man is taught the right lesson, then he dies like a fool. With all the beautiful girls I know . . ." he mumbled. "Why for the devil's sake did I need her companionship? Such a female wolf, it sounds almost like a Red Riding Hood story. Come, dear, I'll tell you a story. She sure did. This is a story I won't forget. . . . *Donner Wetter!*" he cursed.

"Well, Prager," said Bari, "you must know by now who we are. Do you have any suggestions or recommendations as to how you can survive the war and go home?"

Prager said, "You have me. What else do you want from me? You didn't get me over here for advice. All you want is my life in revenge. You've got it. Go ahead—I'm ready, shoot me."

"Look, Prager," said Bari, "you must know by now that you don't deserve to have your life spared, but if you can find an alternative we are willing to listen. We can always shoot you as our last resort, but this isn't what your family would prefer? Or is it?"

With his slit eyes, Prager looked straight at him and said:

"What do you want me to do? Betray my people? Never! You sure don't expect me to win the war for you?"

"No, Prager. We are going to win the war without your help. All we want is your suggestion on how to handle you."

Prager looked up under his raised eyebrows and said:

"Why don't you make a trade with the police? Hand me your radio and I'll talk to them. You have me in custody. They have a few dozen of your people. What if they trade me for all of your captured men. Sounds like a fair deal, doesn't it?"

"Oh, it does," Bari said. "It does." He paused. "Only we are not interested."

"We don't trust you. We are too much in the open, we can trap ourselves very easily with the slightest indiscretion. To have you call on the radio would be like inviting a hundred wolves into a chicken coop."

A half dozen partisans were called into a huddle. The question was: What to do with Prager? Natasha was in on it.

"Watch him, he is very tricky," she said. "He is capable of slipping out and coming back with a motorized Gestapo battalion and chopping us all into pieces."

"Yes, maybe we should just shoot and bury him," someone added. "It's too risky to keep him around for long."

"Sure—he never gave a break to any of our comrades, why should we footsy with him."

"Let's call on the radio station Pobeda (the Russian word for Victory) and ask them for advice," recommended Bari.

167

This received the approval of all. Bari picked up the radio and after several efforts got through.

"Hello, Pobeda. This is Ogon 701." (Ogon is Russian for fire.)

"This is Pobeda, over."

"We caught a carp. What shall we do? Over."

"Hello 701. We'll be there tonight. Guard him with extra caution. Over."

"Yes, comrade, we are waiting. Over."

As it turned dark, they got a chain and lock from Prager's bike and attached it to his foot and to a nearby tree.

"We radioed. Prager, tomorrow you'll be picked up by a unit from the Red Army. You are going to be treated better than you treated us."

Prager remained unimpressed with these assurances. He didn't believe them. What Red troops? As far as he knew the Reds were beaten, and only remnants of diehards were holding out far away in Stalingrad.

Two guards were at Prager's side when the camp retired. Suddenly loud shouts brought the partisans to their feet. It was Prager, screaming out in German: "This is Prager. I'm a prisoner in the woods. Help!"

He explained that he had had a nightmare. No one believed him. He had made a last ditch effort to alarm the *polizai* hoping that his shouts would carry into the village.

Before dawn an odd noise alerted the guards. It was Prager trying unsuccessfully to choke himself with both hands.

It was still dark when the Red Army helicopter arrived. It was nicknamed, Kuritza, the chicken, because of its flopping wings and its sinking style of landing.

A short radio broadcast from the helicopter, a little fire signal from the partisans, and there it was on the ground. A wide door opened, and a man with a flashlight appeared.

"Privet Towaristchy," he greeted. "We brought you medical equipment, food and modern weapons, so you can help us to defeat the enemy quicker. But first, let's meet your catch."

168

"Be my guest," said Bari and four Red soldiers hopped down.

Prager lay, resigned, at the foot of a tree, looking in the opposite direction.

One Russian focused a bright spotlight at the captive's face and took a look at him. "Oh, a German SS officer. We'd like to hear what's new. We already have several hundred of his caliber from Stalingrad. We'll just add him to our collection."

"Allow me to introduce his captor, Natasha, our newest partisan." With a blush on her smiling face, she modestly lowered her head.

"How is the situation in Stalingrad?" people asked.

"Stalingrad is in our hands. The city is all clear of Germans. Now we have got them on the run. Pretty soon, Hitler, kaput."

These last two words were understood by Prager, but he didn't pay attention. He didn't care.

"And now we need a crew of volunteers to unload the goodies."

Except for the guards, everyone climbed into the helicopter and looked at bundles of carefully wrapped supplies in green canvas. There were a couple dozen of those heavy pieces.

"Careful, boys, this is your modern new automatic that catches Fritz in a second."

When the copter was empty, Prager was led inside. The door was locked, a spray of dust followed and it took off.

The partisans stood by, looking on. They knew that soon this bird would return to them with new hope.

Natasha, as the days passed, became acquainted with Aaron. Her thoughts were constantly of David, and something about this Aaron was familiar to her.

But it would be a long time yet before she knew.

15

THAT EARLY MORNING when Bari received a radio order to merge his group with another, Aaron found an old friend.

"They have a more secure location," he told his men, "and we will then be twice as strong."

All the gear was loaded into packs to be carried on the backs of the partisans. Natasha and Nina, too, carried their share. They walked three days. Then, prearranged signals led them to their new camp.

Through a thin screen of woods, partisans were seen cleaning weapons. They stood to greet their new comrades.

"Hey, Aaron," a voice rang out. "Aaron!"

Aaron was stunned by the familiar voice. It was Wladislav, a Polish farmer whom he had once met at Motka's tea house.

"For God's sake, what brought you here, Wladislav?"

"Oh, Aaron, I'm so glad to see you. I'll tell you everything, but first unload your pack and rest up."

The rest of the group was already resting. Some had their boots off and were drying them out in the dry air penetrated with the odor of countless pines.

"Wait, Aaron, and I'll bring you something. Wait, wait."

"I'll wait, I'll wait. I promise you I won't go away," Aaron replied joshingly.

Bread and berries were distributed. Food boxes were opened and distributed evenly to all newcomers. Cold water from a nearby well was brought by the pail. They were emptied by the thirsty partisans as soon as they were set on the ground. Wladislav walked out with a half-full bottle.

"Here, have a swallow of real vodka." Several joined in this celebration: "For our union and victory."

The newcomers soon found out that they were in the right company. This was one of the better armed units. Among them were several Red Army parachutists who had become lost, and several tankists who brought their automatics with them. There were a half dozen young men just coming into military age who had escaped the German forced labor drive. Wladislav was one of a group of Polish Socialist Party members.

Aaron and Wladislav began to refresh each other's memory as to how they met the first time.

"It was on a Friday," Wladislav began, "a winter day with snow way over the knees. I was ordered to harness a horse, hitch him to a wagon, and take the produce to the nearest market for sale. From early dawn I trudged through deep snow with my tired, overworked horse pulling the load of dairy produce for the townspeople.

"My skinny horse, puffing and perspiring, fought the difficult terrain foot by foot. It was pitiful just to watch him suffer. I had a torn sack over my head and bulky, patched-up clothing, and grossly oversized pants, and rags tied around my feet with pieces of rope."

"Yes, I remember," interjected Aaron, "and you looked like a moving sack of potatoes. All that showed from under your makeshift hood was a red and blue nose surrounded by a long mustache covered by icicles.

"As you reached the market you pulled a sack of hay from the wagon, gave the horse a few pats on his steaming back, and spoke to him as if he were a human being.

"Like a thirsty camel after a week's journey, the horse plunged his head all the way into the sack and chewed. I looked at him and thought to myself, 'There is one who

171

works like a horse and eats like a horse.' I saw you hopping around for awhile trying to get more circulation into your feet. You folded your arms in a clap-around, warm-up exercise, calling out: 'Butter, cheese, milk. Right here, folks, fresh from the cow, reasonable. It's cold, come on, I have to get home today, yet.'

"It didn't take you long to sell your supply. By the time my turn came for one liter you said, 'There is an extra quart, have it all. Your luck, young man.'

"I recall how you put the change in a flimsy cotton *babushka* and tied the ends with a knot. You placed it carefully in your deep pants pocket, handed out another few extra love pats to your horse and you asked, 'Where can I get a good hot cup of tea around here that will warm up my intestines.'

"I took you down the steps to Motka's tea house, called the Folks' Delight. These were the quarters where farmers came after everything was sold, but never before, because something might be stolen."

"Yeh," Wladislav went on. "It was a narrow passage hall with chairs along the side of the walls. A few narrow tables had no coverings and insects were all over them. The smoke from a broken iron stove choked the throat and watered the eyes.

"But as frozen as I was, inside, although crowded, dark and stuffy, was a paradise. It was like walking into a little heaven from a big hell. There you introduced me to Motka, the Jewish tea house owner."

"And you got to like him right away," said Aaron. "With a smile showing your buck teeth, you stretched your right hand sideways and into the palm of Motka. Grasping his hand with the two of yours, you said in a slightly excited voice, 'Five and five makes ten, *psia krev*, blood of a dog!' "

"He liked me too," said Wladislav. "Sitting down, he asked me to have a cup of hot tea. On the house!

"He turned the small faucet of an old banged up samovar full of dents, and steaming hot water poured down into a clumsy half mug.

172

"I couldn't wait until the boiling water cooled off. A few quick sips and in no time the tea was all gone. Surprising how I didn't burn my tongue."

"I had to laugh," said Aaron, "when you said, 'Thanks, Motka, that tea just melted my belly button.' Then you both smiled as the conversation went on and on, occasionally interrupted by an outburst of hearty laughter.

"Motka told you a joke, but the noise of the loud customers drowned out his words. Then what happened?" Aaron asked.

"Well, it was time for me to go back to the village. I saw Motka hurrying into the backroom closet and bringing out a couple pairs of old shoes. 'Here, Wladislav, give it to your kiddies, mine grew out of them. At first I didn't want to take it. Motka had so little himself, but when I saw that Motka meant it from the bottom of his heart, I accepted them.

"I remember how you knelt, took Motka's hand and were going to kiss it," said Aaron, "but Motka was embarrassed. He quickly pulled his hand away and said: 'You don't have to do that. Have a good trip.' "

"I never forgot him," continued Wladislav. "During the long trip through the drifting snow I was thinking of that little Jewish stranger, villainized by the *szlachta*. I learned that a mind can be brainwashed, but not a heart. I really miss him. I wonder where he is?"

They stretched out on their backs, looking into the deep sky. The earth smelled of flowers, grass and trees. It gave a promise of warmth, shelter, security and rest. For a while, life acquired another dimension.

"Tell me Wladislav, how did you ever get here?"

"Do you have two days? I'll tell you. When the Germans occupied Vilnius, they picked out the undesirables, unproductives, and many others whom they just didn't like. I was among them. Two *polizai* got me out of bed and took me to the police station. A big fat man shouted to me in Lithuanian. I couldn't understand a word he was saying. I had never learned this language. Enraged and drunk he took his belt off and hit me over my head with the buckle.

I could see sparks flying from my eyes. I staggered and held on to a table.

"He slapped me around a few more times and told me to stand up. He kicked me in my ankle and hollered: 'Go outside. There you'll meet more of your Red comrades.'

"We were sent to a camp. They drove us twelve hours without a stop in back-breaking work. The food consisted of a thin slice of stale bread and soup. It was really hot water with a few rotten potatoes in it. Everyday, people died of starvation.

"I knew my turn would come sooner or later so I decided to make a break. There was less than one chance in a hundred, but at least a chance. I took it without much hesitation.

"Through the whole day's work, I looked for a hideout. I spotted a narrow space between two huge rocks in a stone quarry. I dug a hole under a massive rock, without raising suspicion.

"Shortly before the work day was over, I squeezed inside. I pulled with all my strength on the edge of the rock to cover the hole. Part of this huge stone surface pressed against my shoulder. I had to restrain myself from moaning. During roll call it started to thunder. The Germans were in a hurry to leave. They may have missed calling out my name. As soon as it got dark, I climbed out and waded through the woods. I ate berries and leaves called *stshav*. They are sour but tasty. My mother used to prepare it with sour cream, a wonderful soup. I found an empty sardine can. I straightened out the edges and smoothed them out with a stone.

"Later, when they hunted for me, I submerged in a stream, breathing through a reed until the guards and dogs left.

"There were many days like this, with them hunting and me hiding. But finally I found these good fellows, these partisans, and now I am here."

One dark chilly night the partisans were alerted by radio and ordered to get ready for an offensive. They were ordered to dig in at the outskirts of the forest and wait for further orders.

At dawn, Germans could be seen hurriedly retreating. The poorly armed partisans were no match, and so the order "watch and wait" still stood. Hours later, when light clearly broke through the semi-darkness, *polizai* were seen following their retreating German allies. The bundles of different sizes, shapes, and colors on their backs were a sight to see. Scared of their own crimes, those *polizai* could see themselves dead.

The partisans decided to take a first crack at them.

Hit by cross-fire, the *polizai* were stunned. Caught in the open road without a place to hide, they were shocked by the surprise attack. Their twitching eyes narrowed at the barrage of bullets. One bulky *polizai* fell on his stomach with his huge bag clinging to his back. Several began to run. Surrounded from three sides of the forest, they ran into gunfire and grenades. The *polizai* didn't fire a shot. Those who eluded the bullets made a last effort dash toward the woods only to be nailed down by the attacking partisans.

Finally the *polizai* were laid out flat on the ground. With guns drawn the partisans rushed to take their belongings, mainly their weapons. The badly wounded were given one extra "mercy shot." The rest were tested for fakery.

One of them lay with his face down and not a sound or breath could be heard. Since there was no blood, a partisan kicked him on the side of his stomach. He cried out and opened one eye.

"Get up, you mustached rat, and come with me." He got up slowly with his hands up. Sweat poured from his face under his collar.

"I have never done you any harm," he began to defend himself. "I served in traffic."

"In traffic, ha! Just looking around for our men to turn them in for interrogation before they got shot, ha? We've heard this song before. You're three years too late for it."

The *polizai* was flabbergasted. His face turned red like a beet and his profuse perspiring turned him into a mass of sweaty ugliness. One shot through the back of his head left him lying along with the rest of his fellow traitors.

The partisans gathered near a shortwave transmitter awaiting further orders. The latest news told of more partisan units closing in on the retreating enemy.

"The blitz is turning into a *shvitz*" became the favored motto with the underground men. Courage began to take the place of fear, but caution no one could afford to ignore. Phony orders, likely from the *polizai*, began to join the shortwave messages and partisans had long huddles before they made their next step.

Once, a long panzer tank rumbled through the main road causing the nearby trees to tremble. A grenade was tossed under it; it exploded and the tank caught fire. The chain snapped and the tank crew began to file out, only to be greeted by a hail of bullets.

Orders were beamed to cut off the retreating, lightly armed German and puppet force. People hugged each other and shouted: "Soon the war will be over. We'll be free at last."

The radio beamed: "Comrade partisans. The Nazis are on the run. The Red Army is beating them on all fronts. Together, hand in hand, we'll do our share in defeating our common enemy—the German oppressor and his Ukrainian cohorts. We are going to make them pay for every drop of our people's blood."

The partisans had their best day since the beginning of the war. Close to a hundred enemy were killed and the partisans suffered not one death. They had captured a good number of rifles, pistols and grenades. At times it seemed as if they could use more people to handle all this equipment.

Just when it began to appear that the total initiative was in the hands of the partisans, remnants of the SS Panzer Grenadier Battalion and a detached flame-throwing company emerged. Spotting the partisans, they stopped and after organizing in a "V" formation, began to pour flames on the forest. Soon leaves began to burn and trees went up in smoke.

Caught by surprise, the partisans had no time to dig in.

Their shots bounced off the heavy German tanks like beans off a wall.

The excessive heat from the great fires forced the partisans to retreat deeper into the forest. After securing their pullback, the Germans moved on, kicking up the dust, thus forming a partial smoke screen behind them.

The lightly wounded, those overcome by smoke, those surviving of the underground fighters were the lucky ones. About a third of them didn't make it out of the blazing forest.

The partisans were choking and gagging. The fire caught Aaron's shirt and flared up his back. A coat was thrown over him and he got away with minor burns.

From deep in the forest they watched the fires light up the sky. The shadows of the flames shot upward, raging and crisscrossing and running in wild circles. The fire circled all around. It plunged and rose like a beserk red devil.

Driven by the heat, they decided to leave the forest. They met another unit digging in near a side road, bracing for an attack on the retreating Germans.

After a short consultation between their leaders, they joined forces. Forced away from the woods by a heavy artillery barrage and flame throwers, they took up positions on the outskirts facing a secondary road. Germans avoided taking side roads not shown on their maps. They were warned to stay away from deserted areas where the bandits, as they called the partisans, were in the habit of lurking.

During the night more scattered partisans joined with their arms. Quips about the retreating Germans and the Ukrainian *polizai* running after them like drowning rats dominated the air.

Their jubilation over the retreating Germans was marred by the thought of those who were no longer among them. "We'll never see them again, never talk to them again, and never share their sorrows and joys." Everyone was touched by the loss of dear ones. They had learned to grit their teeth and carry the hatred of their enemy in their hearts.

But it was very hard to accept these losses. They had one aim left—to fight until the end.

Aaron asked himself on one occasion, "I wonder if there is such a thing as a holy war? If there is, then this is it."

The partisans became bolder every day, challenging every retreating German group. Grenades were hurled at trucks, and the troops were peppered with bullets. One sedan received a direct hit by a bullet, and the small passenger automobile was engulfed by streams of fire. Several SS staggered out in panic. They emerged with their hands above their heads, running straight toward the makeshift bunkers. Their shoulder patches showed that one of them was an officer of high rank.

The Germans were stunned at the sight of the approaching partisans. They expected the ambush to come from the regular Russian army. They felt like nothing, surrendering to these filthy and shabbily dressed bandits.

If they had their choice, they would rather have surrendered to a regular army even if it was Russian, rather than a bunch of civilians. Their humiliaton was great and their fear even greater.

They were led away and shot. It was the most frustrating, cruel stage of the war. There was no time for any semblance of a trial. There were no courthouses, no judges, no defenders, no prosecutors, no juries . . . justice flew out of this part of the world as soon as the Germans began to dig their death pits.

Now it was their turn to fill them.

Executions were nothing unusual to the partisans, nor was it considered by them inhuman when they compared the way in which their tortured comrades had died. The name of the game was Revenge. It was based on the concept: "It's either him or me, so I'm going to do everything, no matter what it takes, to get him before he gets me."

No form of execution could be compared with the means which the Nazis had already used.

In the partisans' eyes, quick death by shooting was almost a merciful act.

As the partisans returned to their trenches with guns

over their shoulders, the local inhabitants, who had witnessed the episode, stood by for a few more seconds before they dispersed. A woman went inside a house where her two children were looking out from their beds, and closed the windows.

They had heard about shooting bandits and Reds, but Germans? This was a new experience. For collaborators it was a terrifying time. What would happen when their German protectors were beaten? Over a period of four years, a good number of Ukrainians were convinced by the Germans' rash promises of a Free Ukraine.

There were those who worked wholeheartedly with the Germans, and for the Germans. It reached the point where many truly believed that the future of Germany was theirs.

After years of German occupation many inhabitants who did not want to collaborate with the enemy were sucked in, unwittingly. Some had friends or relatives who had become "involved" and could not help being drawn in by them.

The question was: To what extent could a person avoid cooperation under a forceful occupation of this sort, short of being shot.

Those who didn't escape to join the partisans had no other choice but to obey orders in order to survive.

Young wives with babies, whose husbands were drafted into the Red Army, had hardly any other choice but to stay home, raise the children and hope that someday the Germans would be defeated and their husbands would return to them alive. To them the flicker of hope looked brighter every time a German tank was set on fire.

The turn of the war began to take on a new dimension which affected the future of the Soviet people on both sides of the frontier. As for the Germans, they found themselves harassed on both sides of the front. The population becoming uneasy, nervous, insecure, suspicious, and less dedicated to the "world liberation" policy of Adolph Hitler.

At that stage more former Soviet citizens began to realize that the Nazis hadn't given thousands of their own lives just to give them freedom. Collaborators felt betrayed when the Germans did not help them escape.

For the first time many realized that the Slavs would remain the inferiors in the eyes of "pure aryans" no matter what they did for the Nazis. But it was too late, so they just kept their mouths shut and eyes open looking for a way to escape from their pursuing countrymen.

Aaron together with a small group of co-partisans stayed one whole night in a Ukraine house.

"Prosim, Prosim," a Ukrainian in his fifties bowed with an inviting smile.

"May we consider you then as our friend?" Aaron asked.

"I'm an obedient citizen and I'll do what I'm told."

"What have you been doing under the Germans?"

"I was a teacher of arithmetic. You know, arithmetic knows no politics. As a boy I was taught to love everybody. Maybe this is not so good, but what else could I do. The Russians wouldn't take me into the army because of my bad leg, and how far could I escape by foot. The party members escaped the onrushing Germans in every village vehicle available."

"Is that all you were teaching the kiddies? Arithmetic?"

"That's all, so help me God."

"How much money in taxes did you pay to the Germans?"

"Please boys, have a snack," he said, beginning to set the table with bread and fruits. "Please, *rebiata*, don't ask me so many questions. I have a headache today."

"We suffered plenty. Did we learn our lesson. And how! I hope our children and grandchildren learn it too."

The partisans began to search every house in the community for collaborators. They called it "combing the lice out and squashing the blood suckers."

They went in pairs. Aaron and Wladislav worked as a team. They knocked on the door of the *polizai* chief but got no answer. They pushed the unlocked door open and saw him hanging from a rope. The chief was dressed in his full uniform. His face had blue-grey undertones and his dark hair was draped over his forehead similar to his führer, Adolph Hitler. The chief's face was tragic-grotesque. His

180

pale pink lips were contorted into a sour smile, and a yellow-purple tongue hung out of his mouth.

Aaron took a look at him and said, "For such a savage beast, I won't waste a single unnecessary move."

They walked into the bedroom and found his wife with her hands folded across her breasts, poisoned.

On the night table stood a framed photograph of a young married couple and a child.

"Shall we bury this couple and make it our home for tonight?" Wladislav asked.

"Not a chance," replied Aaron, "I want no part of this damned place. Who wants to sleep in the house of a rotten dog. Let's go on further."

"Where are all your young girls?" Wladislav asked a woman. "The devil knows where they are. Some made love with the S.S. They took off last night. I wonder how far they are going to go in their chase after the Germans?"

Just then two naked young women were seen marching along a sandy road with two farm women following them. Aaron and Wladislav took a look at this unusual scene.

The two naked young people had their hair all shorn and were it not for their breasts, from a distance they could have easily been taken for boys. The two farm women were armed with a pitchfork and a sharp spade.

"There's Tania, the whore," the old woman exclaimed pointing. "The one with the crooked legs. That ugly slut . . . she must have bent them by clinging to the Germans.

"Hey, how about that, the other one is Katska, the no-good. An SS man once told me that she has such a rear that there is enough room for six people to play pinochle on it."

As the four women passed the house, she put her palms to her mouth and asked: "Hey, Sasha Petrovna, where are you taking those two birdies?"

"—To a cage where they can face justice, where else?"

"Hand them over to the partisans," somebody hollered.

An elderly woman with snow white hair hurried up and spat on the girls, right into their faces.

The two girls, seemingly expecting the worst, weren't

shocked by the reaction of their neighbors. They went on, their pale faces sagging.

The partisans walked away. A short distance away a general store was being robbed.

Women and children were grabbing bedding, blankets, linens, coats, dresses, shoes. . . . A small boy was carrying two handfuls of candies, losing a few on the way, to be picked up quickly by a little girl.

The owner, a free enterpriser, had consorted with the Germans, and now the people were getting even with him.

The villagers did their looting undisturbed. A group of partisans stood by and looked on.

Aaron and his partner saw a middle-aged woman patiently digging a shallow hole in her garden. At her feet they saw something shiny. It looked like an old army sword.

"Podruha, ha podruha! What are you trying to hide there?"

"Nothing, nothing, it's none of your concern."

"Oh, yes it is, dearie. What if you decide to dig it up someday and kill us?"

"Me? Kill you? Now why would I do that? It belonged to my grandpa. It's something I want to keep."

"Ladna," Aaron said, "it's okay. You are just lucky you didn't try to hide a rifle. For that we have orders to shoot."

The large friendly landscape soothed the ragged nerves of those young men who had been under a death sentence for years. The quiet, the softness of the panorama whispered beautiful words: "Relax, have peace of mind."

Little farmhouses, haystacks, cows munching on grass, a well where the women pump and hoist up water for their buckets; a little girl standing on a ladder and picking apples from her apple tree; all this spelled tranquility, peace. People minded their own business. They tried to ask as few questions as possible. It was a time of transition; one government goes, another comes. Better to wait another day or two and find out for sure who is going to stay. They refrained from asking: Where do you come from? How long are you going to stay, boys?

There was an old man sitting on the front step of his

tiny house smoking a pipe. He puffed and looked at the strangers without moving an eyelid.

Geese, goats, chickens, pigs, horses, cows; all seemed to be strolling, at peace with themselves and each other. The earth, which offered so much was shared by the animal world. At this point Aaron couldn't resist remarking: "Look, Wladislav, why can't we too live on the riches of this blessed land without hurting each other?"

"You should ask this question of Hitler, if he is still alive," Wladislav replied.

16

GRADUALLY THE PARTISANS disbanded. They left as early as they could, to return to their homes to see what was left of the lives they once knew. As soon as word came that this village or that was liberated, some left. Partings were all the same, joyous and sad. Songs were sung, hands were clasped. Names and faces were pressed into memory, and none would forget.

Natasha and Nina had left.

So had Wladislav.

Aaron stayed on yet, for Vilnius was still in German hands.

His job was processing refugees and questioning suspected collaborators. It was a full time job, full of tension. But it was a different kind of tension than what he had known in the woods.

When the old wall-clock rang four times, he picked up his coat and empty lunch bag and walked to his little castle, a modest but comfortable house that he shared with five other partisans. Every day was the same—a stream of people to question, then the chime of the clock, and another night.

Then, one day he picked up *Pravda* and read the headline he was waiting for.

It screamed, "Vilnius is free!"

He tore out the page of the newspaper, and over the type he wrote:

My Dear Father, Mother and David,

    I am so happy that now we can be reunited. The good Lord has been good to me. I hope He has spared you too.
    I'll write a more detailed letter as soon as I receive your reply.

                    With love,

                    Your Aaron

P. S. It took me four long years to realize how much I really love you.

He put his pen down and wiped the tears away.

The next morning, his co-workers were waiting to congratulate him. Vilnius was not far from the German border, and with Russian troops hammering the Third Reich it looked as if the war was in its final stage. The offensive moved so rapidly that broadcasts came in about every half hour. Enemy military units and their arms were captured. Strategic points and cities were regained one after another.

Sheer optimism drove the people.

Now, day after day, the reports were the same: Russian troops passing through on their way west to Germany; refugees passing east, from somewhere, to find homes they had long fled. They came in streams, both ways, until they all looked alike.

Then, one day as Aaron stood watching them, he stopped, stunned.

That soldier, he looked like David. Something about the eyes, the nose. "I must be tired, my head is spinning." Aaron began to see rings in front of him. For a moment he felt dizzy. He held his head and forced his eyes to open wide. The man did look like his brother. But how could it be?

The partisan stood up and began, uneasily, to move toward the Lieutenant. As he came closer, his eyes flashed and his heart pounded like a cannon.

"David! David!" he shouted hysterically.

David took one look and recognized his brother. The two fell into each others arms.

"Thank God you're alive," David said with a broken voice, full of emotion. Aaron felt like a little boy in the arms of his father. He couldn't speak. This was too much of a surprise. Too sudden. Too unexpected. Up to now nothing had touched him so much. Now he couldn't control himself any longer. For a few moments they shook hands wordlessly. David's eyes were deeply focused on his brother's face. It was happy but wet from tears.

"Sorry, David, a partisan should never cry."

"True, but partisans and soldiers are human beings too."

They both cried.

David wiped his eyes with a wide army handkerchief and dried off Aaron's face. Aaron took it and blew his nose. Embarrassed in the presence of the crowd, they walked away.

The crowd stared. But they understood. Every one of them had lost someone. Maybe this could happen to them someday.

Later, when word of the miraculous reunion had spread, all the partisans and troops were called together.

Colonel Mikhail Derkacz, now in command of both army and partisans in the sector, knew the effect the reunion of David and Aaron would have on his men—and he knew how important it was now to keep up their morale.

How better than to celebrate this great reunion—call all the men together, let them know and feel that it might happen to them, too?

The colonel called all his men into a large barn-like building in which a microphone had been set up. He called Aaron and David up and put his hands on them in a fatherly fashion.

He then turned back to the microphone, and facing the audience said with a slight Ukrainian accent:

"Dear Comrades: Events like this don't happen often. I wish this building were twice as big so twice as many

186

of us could have the privilege to witness this beautiful scene.

"Two brothers, one an officer in the Red Armed Forces, and one a partisan, two members of our heroic forces who crushed the Nazi beast, lost track of each other. Now they have met again and are united."

The two brothers were deeply moved. The Colonel turned to them and said with love and sympathy:

"All right, enough, you two. And that is an order. I'm not an actor and if you keep it up you'll make me cry, too. Imagine, a colonel of a victorious Red Army goes through a war without a single whine, and here, when the war is over and it's high time to be joyful, he takes out a handkerchief and starts weeping."

He pulled out a large handkerchief, and made a sad face. The audience roared.

David and Aaron smiled, not taking their eyes away from each other.

The applause began to grow, and then there were cheers. Spontaneously, several in the audience began to sing, and all joined in:

> *We are with you,*
> *Mother Russia,*
> *All the way*
> *Together with you.*
>
> *When you get hurt*
> *We'll heal your wounds;*
> *When you are poor*
> *Our last shirt*
> *Is for you.*
> *Yes, Mother Russia,*
> *Everything for you.*
>
> *We will not be divided,*
> *Our enemy will fail;*
> *We are strong united,*
> *Hurray! let's hail!*
>
> *So here we stand together*
> *Behind you,*

187

You are not alone;
The whole nation is with you

In pleasure or pain
We are all links
Of one big chain;
For our land
We march hand in hand.

The audience went on clapping in unison in typical Russian fashion as the three headed toward the exit.

Outside, two playful little girls stopped giggling and took a serious look at the colonel clutching the two men. True love and brotherhood could be felt in the air.

Aaron's letter to Vilnius was returned to him. There was an official note on it that his and David's parents had not survived. The details they would find when they got there. But there was no doubt. Their parents had been killed with twenty-one more of their family.

But now finding each other was like wine, and they drank fully of it.

"Yes," said David, "we have learned a big lesson. In the worriless life as kids at home we thought that love, contentment and security were a fixed guarantee. All we had to do was cry and Mom would be right there to wipe our tears. Most requests were promptly granted by Papa."

"How true," Aaron said. "From now on we are on our own. Now there is nothing else but to pick up the pieces and do our best in putting them back together. We just have to do the best we can with the meager crumbs of life handed to us. We'll mold them together into a little loaf with which to feed our injured souls. This is the least the world owes us."

"It owes us nothing. The less we expect, the less we'll be disappointed," David said. "I guess that's how life is; full of ups and downs. We must take what comes and go on.

"You said, 'This is life.' Is it? Why is it that to some life is without trouble and to others only trouble? The way I see it, it is not worth all the suffering.

Understanding his discouragement, David shook his head in agreement, then said, "But there must be more to it. Maybe in time, if we try, we can make life more what we want it to be."

"This is what our parents used to say," Aaron said, "and look how they wound up—cut off from life. Maybe we get just so much time, and when the time expires, life is gone. It isn't how long we live, but what we do with our lives. There are people in this world that no one ever hears about until they die."

"Our parents, whatever has happened to them, live in our hearts."

"Does that mean the two of us are not alone?"

"Exactly, Aaron, and then the time will come when you'll get married, and I'll get married. We'll raise two families and they'll branch out into more families. They will have to grow up without two sets of loving grandparents," he added sadly.

"That's the idea," Aaron said with relief. "Life is like moving upward. It's like climbing up a rugged mountain at times. We slip, tip over, and fall. It hurts, but what can we do? We can't just sit down and cry. One has to get up, straighten out, and keep on moving upwards."

"Yes, David. There is a long hard road ahead of us, but we are going to make it. We lost a bloody battle, but we won the fight for life. It must go on. Our offspring will become our inspiration. We can't let this horror end up without honor. This is no time to feel sorry for ourselves. The whole thing was like a horrible nightmare. Now, we are awake. With our eyes open we have to look for a better future. With our minds free we can search for a happier life.

"It's time to get moving," said David.

He got up first, helped his brother put his meager belongings into the straps of his pack, and began to walk. At the roadside, they saw a small building with people standing in a long line. Its entrance had a sign reading: "Travel Information." A train going in the direction of Vilnius was scheduled to depart in about an hour.

189

People stood grim in silence. A middle-aged man with sagging shoulders and lowered head took an occasional glance backwards, listening in on the two brothers' conversation as if he wished something like that would happen to him.

The man tried to keep from listening, but he couldn't help his curiosity, or perhaps it was his loneliness. He said: "I'm the only one left from my whole family. There were times I wished I was with them. But I guess I was lucky."

David looked at Aaron as if he had in mind to say, "Look, then. We are twice lucky."

"Tell me," said David, "was it worth all this for sweet life?"

The brothers looked at each other.

There was no answer to the question. They had each other. They had the breath of life.

It was worth it.

From behind the grey clouds, the sun appeared. It touched a gloomy world, and Aaron and David began to feel its warmth.

A gentle breeze carried with it a soothing message: "Go home. You'll be needed, you'll be wanted by someone. You may love life again now."

17

NATASHA'S VILLAGE had been destroyed. When she arrived, she walked to where her modest home had stood, looked at what little was left of it, and made her decision.

She must learn something of David. She would go to Vilnius to search for him.

She could not know if he were alive or dead. She did not know where the war had taken him.

But, before she could decide anything of her own future, she must try to find him.

Now she waited in Vilnius.

There were many like her, waiting every day for the right train to arrive and the right person to alight. All day they waited, then again the next day.

She stood out from the rest. Solidly built, with her hair combed up and back, her belt tight at her waist, her boots tall. She looked like a Cossack.

If only she could see him. . . .

She had written many letters, and called at many offices, and finally she had been given word that, when last heard of, David was alive, and was an officer. He would probably be on his way, they told her. So she waited.

There was so much to tell him, so much to share with him.

As if punishing herself, she wouldn't leave her room at

night. She looked out the window. Hundreds of soldiers were returning home, some taller than David, some better looking, but none were David.

His voice kept ringing in her ears: "True, Natasha, it is a cruel world, but it is not the end of the world."

Yes, he had wisdom, he had foreseen that they would meet again. That it was meant to be. "I wonder if he misses me. Maybe he is married? I hope not. But if he is, I couldn't blame the girl."

Whenever an army truck pulled up at the corner and stopped, she said, "What if David is in it? I'll die."

Always well groomed, with a slight touch of lipstick and powder on her face, she awaited David daily at the railway station.

Then, the right day and the right train arrived.

First she saw Aaron, the partisan, and was thunderstruck. How much like David, he looked. She ran, then stopped. She stood there, shaking.

Then David stepped off the train behind Aaron.

"David!" she screamed with all her might, as she saw the real David in uniform, his long nose, his bright face, "David! David!"

David just managed to open his arms, and she was inside them, all of her.

Aaron stood for awhile watching the two clasped in a tight embrace. David released his right hand to reach into his pocket for a handkerchief.

"Natasha, I want you to meet my brother, Aaron," said David while wiping away her tears.

Happily she grasped his hand with both of hers and shook it up and down in country style.

"I know! I know!" she said, laughing and crying.

She took both brothers by the arm, holding them tight to her.

Then the three heroes marched off, until they melted into the crowd.

192